"Worth a read among the traditional cozies: Wendy Tyson's *Seeds of Revenge*."

— Marilyn Stasio, *New York Times Book Review*

"Tyson gives us an evocative sense of place, a bit of romance, and dimensional characters with interesting backstories. Readers are left looking forward to the next book in the series and hankering for organic mushroom tartlets."

— *Publishers Weekly*

"This third series offering is a complex small-town mystery with well-rounded, fascinating characters."

— *Library Journal*

"A warmhearted mystery with an irresistible cast of characters, two- and four-legged alike. Tyson's small-town setting is a lush bounty for the senses, and the well-structured plot will keep you guessing right up until the satisfying conclusion."

— Sophie Littlefield,
Edgar-Nominated Author of *The Guilty One*

"Tyson grows a delicious debut mystery as smart farmer-sleuth Megan Sawyer tills the dirt on local secrets after a body turns up in her barn. You won't want to put down this tasty harvest of a story."

— Edith Maxwell,
Agatha-Nominated Author of *Murder Most Fowl*

"Hungry for a great mystery? *A Muddied Murder* is a delight and Wendy Tyson is a natural. She delivers a perfectly plotted mystery with well-planted clues and a healthy dose of secrets. This first Greenhouse Mystery will only whet your appetite for more."

— Sparkle Abbey,
Author of *Raiders of the Lost Bark*

"Tyson's first-rate second Greenhouse mystery stars big-city lawyer turned small-town organic farmer Megan Sawyer, a kind, intelligent, and spirited woman with great integrity. In short, she's the sort of person cozy readers warm to and root for."

— *Publishers Weekly* (starred review)

"Tyson's third look at the joys and perils of small-town life features enough engaging characters."

— *Kirkus Reviews*

"An exceptional cozy, *Bitter Harvest* offers up a veritable feast for mystery fans: a beautifully drawn setting, engaging characters, and plenty of twists and turns that will keep readers guessing. The suspense deepens with every scene...Tyson has crafted a fresh, intelligent, compelling story that's sure to satisfy."

— Cynthia Kuhn,
Agatha Award-Winning Author of *The Art of Vanishing*

"An irresistible story with delicious food, scheming villagers, and a secret worth killing for. Her heroine, prodigal daughter of Winsome, PA Megan Sawyer, may not carry a gun, but she's packing brains, courage, and loads of integrity. Megan is a star."

— James W. Ziskin,
Anthony Award-Nominated Author of the Ellie Stone Mysteries

"Complex characters, interesting twists, and a charming setting add up to a satisfying mystery."

— *Publishers Weekly*

"Wendy Tyson has a background in law and psychology, which lends itself nicely to her endeavors as a crime fiction novelist...Cunning crimes, charismatic characters, and a cozy (if occasionally murderous) community all set this series, and story, apart—as does the authenticity and assuredness with which the author writes."

— *Criminal Element*

Sowing Malice

The Greenhouse Mystery Series
by Wendy Tyson

A MUDDIED MURDER (#1)
BITTER HARVEST (#2)
SEEDS OF REVENGE (#3)
ROOTED IN DECEIT (#4)
RIPE FOR VENGEANCE (#5)
SOWING MALICE (#6)

Sowing Malice

GREENHOUSE
mysteries

WENDY TYSON

HENERY PRESS

Copyright

SOWING MALICE
A Greenhouse Mystery
Part of the Henery Press Mystery Collection

First Edition | July 2020

Henery Press, LLC
www.henerypress.com

All rights reserved. No part of this book may be used or reproduced in any manner whatsoever, including internet usage, without written permission from Henery Press, LLC, except in the case of brief quotations embodied in critical articles and reviews.

Copyright © 2020 by Wendy Tyson
Author photograph by Ian Pickarski

This is a work of fiction. Any references to historical events, real people, or real locales are used fictitiously. Other names, characters, places, and incidents are the product of the author's imagination, and any resemblance to actual events or locales or persons, living or dead, is entirely coincidental.

Trade Paperback ISBN-13: 978-1-63511-627-4
Digital epub ISBN-13: 978-1-63511-628-1
Kindle ISBN-13: 978-1-63511-629-8
Hardcover ISBN-13: 978-1-63511-630-4

Printed in the United States of America

For Ian and Mandy,
who always make me laugh.

ACKNOWLEDGMENTS

Special thanks to....

My wonderful agent, Frances Black, who has stood by me every step of the way and who has made this series possible.

Kendel Lynn and Art Molinares at Henery Press, who gave Megan and Bibi a home.

My husband, Ben Pickarski, for his endless patience with deadlines, book events, and farming questions.

Rachel Jackson for her sharp eye and careful editing.

Stephanie Wollman, for her willingness to answer all of my medical questions.

Ian, Mandy, Matthew, and Jonathan for all of their support— online and offline.

Dru Ann Love, for being such a wonderful champion of the mystery writing community.

Cynthia Bayer Blain and Sue Norbury, for going above and beyond to support this series.

All of the readers, reviewers, fellow authors, and friends of the mystery community. Writing this series has been a dream come true, and I have appreciated all of the support and encouragement along the way.

One

If Winsome was reeling from a death in her midst, you wouldn't know it, Megan thought. The stores and attractions were abuzz with summer activity, locals and tourists alike enjoying a taste of the warm Pennsylvania countryside. The normally quiet roads were alive with traffic, and as Megan made her way along Canal Street in the center of town, walkers, runners, and everything in between were making happy use of the town's main amenity— the canal path. The only sign of the big memorial service scheduled for the top of the hill later that day was the number of cars parked outside of J.M. Morton's Funeral Home.

Even inside Merry's Flowers, with clouds pressing down outside, promising rain, there was a feeling of lightness in the air. Megan grabbed the potting soil her grandmother, Bonnie "Bibi" Birch, had asked for and made her way to the register. She was due to meet with her contractor at two o'clock, and she was in a hurry to pay and get back to the farm. Megan had depended on there being no line at Merry's—which was usually the case. Today, as luck would have it, she had to wait.

Three women, all dressed from head to toe in designer black, stood at the register, waiting while Merry finished tying a white ribbon around a generous bouquet of blooms: white orchids, white lilies, and white irises interspersed with pale, blush-colored roses. The youngest of the group, a tiny brunette with mascara streaks marring sculpted cheekbones, was sobbing, her hip wedged against the wooden counter for support. The other two—an older woman with a sharp-edged platinum bob and a tall woman with a helmet of bottle-red hair—hovered over her with a mix of empathy, concern, and growing impatience.

Megan watched the scene unfold with an outsider's eye.

"Claire, you can't show up like this," Red whispered—loudly. "You *need* to pull yourself together."

Platinum nodded. "My god, she'll eat you alive. *Please.* Stop crying."

Merry Chance, the store's proprietor and a woman known as much for her nosiness as her green thumb, paused to observe the crying woman over fuchsia spectacles. She caught Megan's eye before saying, "I'm sorry for your loss."

The sobbing woman didn't react. Instead, Platinum said, "Do you sell cards as well?"

Merry pointed to a rack of greeting cards. "Sympathy cards are on the top."

Platinum grabbed her crying companion and pulled her toward the cards. Despite the older woman's hushed pleas, the younger woman remained inconsolable. She stared at the cards, clearly uncomprehending.

Merry finished the bouquet and tapped away at the register. "Will they be purchasing a card?" she asked Red.

The woman glanced nervously toward the other two women. "Are you getting a card?" she asked. When Platinum's only response was an exasperated glare, Red smiled apologetically at Merry. "Just the flowers for now...well, you can see she's having a very hard time deciding."

"That's not a problem," Merry said.

Red paid for the flowers, and Platinum started to pull her

charge toward the front of the store. Mid-step, the younger woman crumpled to the ground in a heap of Gucci and Prada. Megan dropped the heavy bag of potting soil and rushed to help her.

"Claire's fine, she's fine," Platinum said, waving Megan away. "She just needs some fresh air."

The woman named Claire didn't *look* fine. She looked like she'd watched one hundred horror movies back to back, and Megan said as much. But Red came over to help, too, and the two women pulled the younger one to her feet. After a moment of confusion, Claire resumed her crying. As the three women left the store, the cries turned to silent, shoulder-heaving sobs.

Feeling a deep wave of sympathy, Megan watched them get into their car through the shop's window. She plopped the potting soil on the counter, her focus still on the women.

"Wonder what that was all about," Merry said. "One thing's for certain, they're not from around here. Did you see the cut of the tunic on the brunette? That was no outlet find." She shook her head. "No, not from Winsome. I'd remember the clothes."

"Must be the von Tressler memorial," Megan said. She pulled a credit card from her wallet and slipped it into the reader, chip first. "They're probably here to pay respects to David von Tressler. His service was this morning."

Merry's eyes widened. "Yes! Visiting Melanie to pay their condolences. Why didn't I think of that? Oh, I know. Because we're never invited to anything at the von Tressler estate, so why *would I* think of that?" Merry's ageless face was a mask of indignant disgust. "Moving here, thinking they're better than us—"

Megan bit her lip in an effort not to smile. No one did righteous indignation quite like Merry Chance.

"*Some people,*" Megan said.

"Some people is right. Why did they even move to Winsome? Who bothers coming to a close-knit community if you're only going to wall yourself off from everyone?"

"The von Tresslers have not exactly reached out to the townspeople, have they?" An understatement, Megan knew. When Melanie and David von Tressler completed the giant home on the hill overlooking Winsome a few months ago, many speculated about why such a wealthy couple would choose this small Bucks County town. Sure, the schools were good. And the town was convenient to Philadelphia and New York City. And for many, the slower pace beat the frenetic feeling of city life. But from what she could tell, neither of the von Tresslers worked outside that mansion, and their only son was a grown man.

Megan had heard the rumors—everything from "they want to get away from the big city," to "they're running from someone," to gossip about deadly accidents and affairs and deceased relatives. Winsome was a small town, and like small towns everywhere, people talked—whether they knew what they were talking about or not.

Every time Megan had stopped by the nursery since the von Tresslers began construction, Merry had been openly aghast at the lack of neighborliness the couple showed: declining her repeated invitations to dinner and fundraisers, and never once frequenting her store. Merry's skin was butterfly-wing thin, but she had a point. The von Tresslers had been standoffish. Megan found them a curious family. A husband, a younger wife, a solitary son, and a house that could shelter ten families. Why Winsome, indeed.

"Cremated the body. I heard he had a heart attack," Merry said.

"That's what I heard, too." Megan glanced back outside, but

the women were no longer there. "Sudden and deadly."

"And now people are showing up to mourn. I wonder who that young woman was. A niece, perhaps? Or maybe an estranged daughter from another marriage. It was a fall/spring marriage, after all." Merry shrugged. "With all that money, I'm sure the memorial service will be extravagant."

While Merry rambled on about the alleged von Tressler fortune, Megan thought about the sobbing woman, her obvious misery. "My god, she'll eat you alive," one of the women had said in an effort to halt the tears. Who would eat her alive, Megan wondered? Melanie von Tressler? Megan thought so—and not because this Claire was a niece or even an estranged daughter. No, if Megan had been a gambler, she'd say there was more to Claire and David than blood relation. Those tears were rooted in the kind of grief one feels when they lose a partner. Megan understood. She'd lost her soldier husband, Mick Sawyer, when they were just starting married life together, and the grief was always there. A persistent, deep ache.

David von Tressler had meant something to the designer-wearing Claire. Something, perhaps, that Melanie von Tressler wouldn't appreciate. But Megan wouldn't say that to Merry. No use feeding the storm of gossip enveloping the von Tresslers. Instead, Megan picked up her potting soil and slung it over her shoulder. The reality of her days involved farm work, animal husbandry, renovating the adjoining Marshall property, and keeping the café afloat. Right now she had a farmers market to prepare for. She had little time for people who had little time for the people of Winsome.

Merry, whose fuchsia-colored glasses now hung from a lanyard around her neck, frowned. "Are you going to the memorial reception?" Merry asked.

Surprised by the question, Megan shook her head. "Why

would I? I only met David and Melanie a few times. We weren't exactly friends."

"They are part of our community."

Megan smiled. It hadn't sounded that way a moment ago. "I'm busy. Plus, I don't think it's open to the public, and I wasn't invited."

Merry must have heard the unspoken "nor were you" because she frowned and turned away to look out the window. "You must be curious, Megan. After all, they did steal your contractor. And every contractor within a twenty-mile radius."

"No time to be curious."

"Always business with you. Where's the joy in that?"

"If there was no joy in it, I wouldn't do it," Megan said.

Merry faced Megan. Her eyes looked sad, burdened even. "There's more to life than Winsome, Megan. Don't you want to know how the other half live?"

"I've had a few glimpses, and I remain unimpressed. Have a good day, Merry."

Megan walked out of the nursery feeling lower than she had when she'd arrived. Her words had been true. She loved what she did and didn't begrudge the rich von Tresslers—or anyone else. It had taken a long time to feel comfortable returning to Winsome, but now that she had, she had everything she needed right here. Still...the women, the grief, Merry's sadness all coalesced into a gut-punch of dread.

Outside, the sky had taken on a brooding character. Clouds assembled overhead, their dark edges portents of the storms to come. Megan tossed the potting soil into the truck's toolbox and climbed into the cab. So much for sunshine. As she started the truck's engine, it started to drizzle, the kind of steamy drizzle that provided no relief to the summer heat.

Before she could leave Merry's parking lot, the rain was

pounding down in unrelenting streams. Her windshield wipers were ineffective, and as she drove slowly down the road, she almost missed the Lexus with Connecticut plates parked along the road next to Merry's Flowers. In it sat a red head, a platinum blond, and a brunette. From the looks on their faces and the angry gestures they were making, they were in the midst of a heated exchange. Based on the flat tire on the passenger side of the vehicle, if they were headed to the von Tressler memorial, they would be very late.

Megan pulled alongside the car. Red opened the window enough to talk with her, and Megan asked if they needed assistance. "I can help you put on your spare."

They looked at each other uneasily before Platinum finally spoke. "We called Triple A." She tapped the windshield. "With this rain, no way we're getting out of the car."

"Suit yourselves." Megan had started to roll her window back up when Platinum waved excitedly at her. She made a rolling motion with her hand, and Megan eased the window back down.

"On second thought, do you think you could give Claire a ride? She needs to be somewhere by two. We tried Lyft but that'll take another eighteen minutes just to get to us."

Megan glanced at the clock on the dashboard. 1:53. She also needed to be somewhere by two, but she *had* offered to help. "Sure," she said.

Claire leaned over. Her eyes, while still wet, seemed clearer. "Thank you. It means a lot."

"No problem."

While Megan waited for her guest to get situated in the truck, she called Ryan, her contractor, to say she'd be late. He sounded annoyed, and she didn't blame him. Time was money— and eventually she would run out of both when it came to fixing up the old Marshall property.

"Thanks again," the woman said. "In case you haven't figured it out already, I'm Claire."

"Megan Sawyer. Where are we headed?"

The woman read her an address from her phone.

"The von Tressler estate?" Megan asked.

The woman nodded. Tears once again sprouted from round green eyes, but the woman seemed to do a better job this time of holding them back.

"You knew David, then," Megan said. "Family?"

Claire didn't answer. She turned her head to look out the window, her slim frame huddled against the seat. The rain had slowed, but thunder boomed, and the darkening clouds continued to gather overhead. Megan was worried about the damage the storms would do to her fields. And while tornadoes were rare in eastern Pennsylvania, they weren't unheard of. Bibi had said just this morning that this was tornado weather. She'd been through enough growing seasons to know.

"Yes, I knew David," Claire said finally. She offered no more.

Megan turned the truck past her own road and kept going, up toward the mansion overlooking the town center. Perhaps she'd probed her passenger enough. It was none of her business after all.

The memorial had brought visitors from the tri-state region, and parking attendants and valets were outside in suits and clear raincoats, directing traffic and parking vehicles. Megan pulled into the circular driveway in front of the Greek Revival house and waited to drop her charge off at the double-doored entrance, one in a long line of mourners.

Thunder boomed again, and Claire jumped. "Sorry," she mumbled. She looked at Megan with downcast eyes. Her once carefully coifed hair hung limply against hollow cheekbones. She'd managed to clean up the mascara, but her eyes appeared naked and sad. Megan noticed slender fingers, unpolished nails chewed down to the quick. "I'm obviously rattled," she said.

"It's okay."

"David...well, I'm not ready to say good-bye."

"He must have meant a lot to you." A parking attendant waved, and Megan pulled forward, in front of the house's entrance. She shifted into park to let the woman out.

"For a while, he was my world. He still should be."

The parking attendant opened the truck door and said, "Name?"

"Mrs. Claire von Tressler."

Claire must have read the confusion on Megan's face because she said, "I told you I knew David." She grabbed her purse and the flowers from the divider between them. Closing her eyes for a split second, she seemed to careen backward, into the seat. When she opened them again, she pushed herself out of the vehicle with weary resignation.

"Wish me luck," Claire said.

"Good luck."

Claire von Tressler disappear into the house, looking tiny and lost against the larger-than-life background.

Two

Megan had arrived home to find the contractor busy, so she went down to the old farmhouse to change into work clothes before returning to her farm chores. In the kitchen, Bibi was stirring a pot of vegetable soup and scolding Sadie, Megan's dog, for begging.

"Now be a good girl," Bibi murmured.

"Bibi, when we met David and Melanie, did they introduce themselves as a married couple?"

Bibi looked up and frowned. "David and Melanie?"

"Yes. The von Tresslers."

Bibi gave the soup another stir and put the wooden spoon on a trivet on the counter. Smells of onions and home baked bread wafted through the warm room. Megan's stomach rumbled. She'd forgotten to eat lunch again. Lately, worries over the Marshall house renovations and their dwindling bank accounts had been keeping her up all night and stealing her appetite.

"Bibi?" When Bibi still looked perplexed, Megan said, "The house you called a monstrosity."

"Ah, now I remember. The old man and his child bride." She tossed a piece of bread to Sadie.

"That's why she begs, you know," Megan scolded.

"Nonsense." Bibi tossed her another piece of bread. "She's a good girl."

Megan threw up her hands in frustration. Bibi would do what she wanted. "The von Tresslers," Megan said again. "They came into the café one day and ordered nothing but coffee, then complained that it was too strong—remember? You were talking to them. Did they say they were married?"

Bibi's face scrunched in concentration. In her mid-eighties, she was a study in motion—most of the time. Today she looked tired, mirroring how Megan felt. Bibi's short hair was curled slightly from the humidity, and she wore a "Winsome Cooks" apron over a striped shirt dress. Sneakers adorned her small feet. Megan felt a surge of love for her grandmother, the most steady person in her life. Aside, perhaps, from Megan's boyfriend, Winsome veterinarian Dr. Daniel "Denver" Finn.

"I remember they sat side by side despite having a perfectly good chair across the table. I remember his hands all over her, and I recall that she seemed to neither invite nor dissuade his attention. I recall that they bickered. Then they complained the coffee was too strong, I offered another cup, and they asked for tea. When they left, they paid only for the tea—despite drinking the coffee, too—and left a fifty-cent tip." She cocked her head. "How's that for a memory?"

Megan smiled. "Pretty darn good. Married?"

"They said they were new in town and lived on the hill. Never specifically called themselves married. Why?"

Megan told her grandmother about the scene at Merry's shop and the ride to the von Tressler memorial reception. "I met the von Tresslers at the café as well," Megan said. "It was a while ago. They were building the house and had come to town to check on the progress. David was gracious but standoffish. Melanie didn't speak except to ask where the restroom was. I saw them later, in town." Megan thought back to that day. Why this was bothering her, she wasn't sure—other than the fact that the von Tresslers had usurped all of the good construction crew in the area, including her original contractor, and she was left with a barebones firm from nearby Doylestown.

"Well, they have no time for us, we have no time for them. Anyway, I heard the woman might be moving now that the husband has passed."

"What about the son?"

"What son?" Bibi asked. "There is no son. No children at all."

"Hmm. I thought I saw them with a son the day they came to check on construction. At least I assumed it was their son." But then, I also assumed Melanie was his wife, Megan thought. Just then, her cell phone beeped. She had a text from Ryan, the contractor. "Ryan's ready for me," Megan said. "If you need me, I'll be up at the Marshall house."

"It's our house now, you know. No need to call it the Marshall house." Bibi sliced a piece of bread, slathered about a pound of butter on it, and stuffed half in her mouth. When Megan glared—Bibi had high cholesterol—Bibi shrugged and smiled.

"Yes, we should call it something else." *But we never will.* The house had been dubbed "the Marshall house" years ago, after it was abandoned by a previous owner. The nickname had stuck. Megan sighed. Pulling on a pair of old sneakers, she glanced again at her grandmother. "You're impossible, you know."

"I think these days I'd be called strong and independent."

Megan laughed. As usual, her grandmother was right.

It took Megan a few minutes to get up to the property that

abutted Washington Acres Farm. The field between the two properties was muddy and rutted, and Megan had to watch where she was walking. The rain hadn't helped matters, and the cuffs of Megan's pants were soaking wet.

The Marshall property constituted an abandoned historic home situated on a large triangular plot of land that bordered state forest on one side, a road on another, and Washington Acres on the third. Long empty, with significant weather and foundation damage, it had been a beast to restore.

Megan and Bibi wanted to make it into an inn and sustainable agricultural learning center for the farm. Last year when renovations began, their original contractor ran into costly and time-consuming issues. Rather than spend the time and money then, they'd opted to construct the new barn on the property, which was to house not only plantings and equipment but would also be a commercial kitchen suitable for classes and events. The barn was mostly finished and ready for action; the house was in its last stages of completion.

Had it not been for Melanie and David, the whole thing would be finished by now—and bringing in money. When the von Tresslers began their project, they tempted away local contractors with lucrative offers. The loss of Duke Masterman, her prior contractor, had been a blow. Now the Marshall project—which had been slated to open in April—had been delayed until July. And once again there were problems, one of which Ryan wanted to discuss today.

Ryan Craig was a tall, muscular man in his forties, with ruddy, tan skin and squinty blue eyes. Megan spotted him standing in the field behind the Marshall house. He and a member of his crew were staring across the field, at the overgrown weeds and wildflowers that had been allowed to grow during the years the house sat abandoned.

"Ryan," Megan said as she approached. "Is now a good time?"

"It'll do." He pointed at the field. "We found some issues with the plumbing."

"What do you mean by 'issues'?"

Ryan's gaze traveled across the property. "We had to dig up the septic tank, which is out there, under that mess. Wanted to let you know because it means delays, and money. Wanted to see what you wanted to do."

Megan eyed the disaster of a yard. The mess could be cleaned up, but septic issues were often expensive. "Do I have a choice?"

"Not really." He shared a litany of concerns about the current plumbing and the septic tank. Although not an expert, Megan agreed with his assessment. She just wished he'd uncovered a cheaper problem.

"Look," he said with empathy in his eyes, "I can have my men dig up the old pipes out to the tank. We won't call in the experts until we absolutely need them. May take an extra day or two, but with this rain, we can only do so much anyway. We'll try to keep costs—and yard damage—to a minimum."

Megan thanked him. While he returned to his crew, she surveyed the property. Once the Colonial was finished, it would be modest but lovely—an open reception area featuring local materials and art, three guest bedrooms with en-suite bathrooms, and a beautiful innkeepers' quarters. They already had people inquiring about staying there. Together with the teaching barn and the pizza farm they'd opened last year, they could offer comfortable rooms, farm-to-fork food, cooking classes, and even the "true farm" experience for those who wanted it. Megan would maintain the organic café and small store in town, and eventually—fingers crossed—they'd be firmly in the black. It would be a dream come true for her, for Bibi, and for Megan's farm manager, Clay Hand. But a lot had to be done before they could get there. Like new plumbing.

For now, she'd take one day at a time.

Denver called later that evening. "I've finished rounds, Megs, and if you can stand the smell of horses on my clothes, we could meet for some dinner and a pint. What do ye think?"

Denver was originally from Scotland, and while his brogue had diminished over time, it became more pronounced when he was tired or agitated. Today he sounded tired.

"I think that sounds wonderful."

"I hear there's a beautiful organic café on Canal Street, and it serves amazing food."

Megan laughed. She loved her café, Washington Acres Larder & Café, but she liked to sample other restaurants during her down time. "I have a better idea. There's a new Indian restaurant on Route 611. Saffron Palace. Want to try that? I hear biryani and cold beer go well together."

"Give me thirty minutes to scrub my hands and wash my face, and I'll be there to pick you up."

Saffron Palace was aglow with gold-filtered lighting and gold-embroidered tablecloths. Megan and Denver sat across from each other in a corner table by a window that overlooked a small, garden-filled courtyard. The scents of cumin and ginger wafted from the kitchen. Megan ordered vegetable biryani and found it did indeed go well with a cold beer. Denver picked at his chicken jalfrezi, seeming to prefer the brew to the food.

"You don't like it?" Megan asked.

"It's delicious. Spicy, but delicious." He glanced toward the entrance where the hostess was seating a party of six. "Just a long day."

Megan put her fork down. "Anything in particular?"

"Normal stuff, plus Mrs. Jaffrey's pet raccoon ate her wedding ring." He smiled. "That was fun. Why you should never have a pet raccoon."

"I didn't know Mrs. Jaffrey even *had* a pet raccoon."

"Neither did Mr. Jaffrey. That was the fun part."

The waitress came with another round of beers, and Megan took a slow sip. "I had an interesting day, too." She told Denver about her contractor's plan. "Thousands more, I'm sure—and additional delays."

"Damn the von Tresslers and their expensive construction projects. But it sounds like you would have had this issue eventually. At least the ground isn't frozen, and Ryan can take care of the problem, so that's good."

"True. Speaking of the von Tresslers, I took a ride up to their house today. Drove Mrs. von Tressler to David's memorial reception."

Denver scooped up some chicken with a piece of roti and shot Megan a questioning look. "Why did you have to drive Melanie to her husband's memorial?"

"Not Melanie." She shared her interaction with the three women. "A woman who introduced herself as 'Mrs. von Tressler.' Maybe David's ex-wife?" Megan flashed a sly smile. "Or perhaps she was his current wife."

"Then who is Melanie? His girlfriend?" Denver shook his head. "A little too modern for my taste."

Megan laughed. "Same here. I'm starting gossip, though. The truth is, I don't know which one was David's wife, if either. Or who is the mother of David's son."

Denver stopped chewing. "David has a son?"

Megan nodded. "A young guy. Looks just like a younger , shorter version of David. At least I assumed he was their son."

"I think ye assumed wrong, Megs. When David took his bonnie little Cavalier to me last month, I asked him about kids and he said he was childless."

"Maybe it's her son. Although she looks way too young to have a young adult son."

Denver shrugged. "Maybe, but people have all kinds of work done these days. I was worried about kids in the house because of the dog's condition, and David very firmly assured me there was no one other than him and Melanie in the house, so I didn't need to worry."

Megan thought about this. She pictured what she'd witnessed between the family members. Melanie with her hand on the younger man's arm. David, looking far older than Melanie, putting a fatherly arm around the man. The trio had been huddled together, talking quietly amongst themselves on Canal Street, by the path. She'd assumed they were family. It was, of course, possible she'd misinterpreted what she'd seen— projected her expectations onto her neighbors.

Megan took a last bite of biryani, savoring the flavors, appreciating the contrasting textures and bold spices. Everything about David and Melanie had seemed flavorless. From the bland but sprawling estate, to their matching silver BMWs, to the noncommittal way they interacted with the townspeople of Winsome. There was a lack of energy and imagination.

"I heard David had a heart attack," Megan asked. "Have you heard the same?"

"Only gossip. Mr. Jaffrey said David had a heart attack. Your aunt Sarah said natural causes. Millie Dunast said he had a tooth infection that went septic." Denver shot her that dimpled grin she'd fallen in love with. "And Ben Biggs said David von Tressler is still alive and this is all a big show to collect his insurance money."

"Well, Ben Biggs wins for creativity."

"Aye, and for not paying his bills on time."

They both laughed. The door to the restaurant opened, and out of the corner of her eye, Megan spotted two of the women from Merry's shop enter. "Don't look," she whispered, "but Claire von Tressler's two friends just arrived."

As soon as the women spied Megan, they high-tailed it to her table.

"Have you seen—" Red said.

"Where is Claire?" Platinum shouted.

Megan stood. "Ladies, please, one at a time. What's wrong?"

It was Platinum who spoke first. "Claire. Where did you leave her?"

"At the memorial," Megan said.

Red shook her head. "She never arrived."

Megan glanced at Denver, who looked as confused as Megan felt. "I dropped her off there myself. Along the circular driveway. I saw her enter the house."

"No one has seen her." Red crossed her arms over her chest. "She's not answering her phone."

"I don't know what to tell you," Megan said. "Maybe she wandered off. She seemed upset. Maybe she couldn't bring herself to go in and went for a walk instead."

Red and Platinum looked at one another. Finally, Red sighed. "Claire's not in a good space right now. We should have been with her. When we arrived and couldn't find her, we went back to the flower shop. The woman there gave us your name.

Your grandmother told us where you were."

Megan's stomach knotted at the thought of strangers talking to Bibi, at the idea of people tracking her down during her date with Denver. She stared down at her hands and saw they were clenched into fists. Too many bad things had happened in Winsome for Megan to feel otherwise.

Denver stood. He towered over the women. "We understand you're worried, but it's the police you need to be talking with, not Megan. The chief's name is Robert King. Give the station a call."

The blond nodded. The redhead looked about to say something but didn't. Denver sat back down.

"I'm sorry," Red said finally. She directed her words at Megan. "But it seems like you were the last person to see Claire, so we didn't know where else to go."

"The police," Megan repeated Denver's words. "I dropped her off at the memorial. Where she went from there, I have no idea."

The two women walked toward the restaurant's exit, their posture lending them a dejected air. Megan saw Platinum glance back, eyes pressed into a ferocious glare.

"Are ye alright, Megs?" Denver asked.

Megan took a deep breath, pushing the women out of her mind. She had done nothing to deserve their anger. Nevertheless, she couldn't shake a strange feeling that she was missing something, that she'd been through this before.

"I'm fine," Megan said. "Fine enough to order another beer. And maybe some dessert."

"Why did you tell those women where we were?" Megan asked her grandmother later that night. It seemed an odd action for a woman who tended to her privacy with more vigor than she watched over her flower gardens—and those flower gardens were spectacular.

"The woman who called—I think she said her name was Penny—was so upset, Megan. Crying. And you had told me all about what happened, so I figured it would be fine." Bibi was sitting in the room she called the parlor, on her couch with knitting on her lap. She looked up and frowned. "Should I not have said anything?"

"No, no...it's fine. I was just surprised to see them, that's all." Megan sat down on the chair across from her grandmother.

"Where is she?" Bibi asked.

"Where is who?"

"The woman who disappeared."

Megan waved her hand. "I'm sure she's turned up by now."

Bibi returned to her knitting. Attention on her work, deep lines around her eyes creased further by worry, she said, "I don't know. Woman turns up in Winsome, disappears. Now her friends are left searching." She glanced up but avoided Megan's steady gaze, staring instead at the darkness outside the parlor window. "The older I get, the less faith I have in humankind. Sometimes there's simply evil in the night."

"You watch too much television," Megan said, standing up. A chill ran through her. Nerves, she thought. She would finish the evening chores and turn in herself. "Not everything ends in drama."

Bibi didn't respond. Megan left the room with her grandmother still looking out the window. At what, Megan didn't know. Clouds were blanketing a quarter moon, and night was absolute.

Three

"Bobby's looking for you," Clover Hand said. "Stopped by about an hour ago. Said he'd head up to the farm."

Megan was lugging a case of onions from the farm into the Washington Acres café's kitchen. She paused to speak to her store manager. Clover was not only sister to Megan's farm manager, Clay Hand, but live-in girlfriend to the town's young police chief, Bobby King.

"Do you know what Bobby wanted?"

"No idea." Clover's long, dark hair had been pulled back into a loose chignon, and she wore a pair of pale linen pants and a clingy navy blue top. Taking the onions from Megan, she nodded toward the café's dining area and the store beyond. "He seemed agitated, but then again, he left before breakfast this morning." Clover smiled. "You know how Bobby likes his breakfast."

Megan's mind flitted back to Claire and her friend. "Did he say anything about a missing woman?"

Clover had already disappeared into the pantry closet with onions. When she returned, she rubbed her hands on a cloth hanging against the wall and shook her head. "Nothing. He woke up, looked at his phone, took a few calls, grunted a good-bye, and left. We have a very romantic relationship, as you can see."

Megan laughed, but the sound was forced, even to her own ears. Bobby King was typically the harbinger of bad news, and Winsome had had its share of bad news in the last few years.

Clover rose on tip toes to look into a large pot on the stove. The café's chef, Alvaro Hernandez, a man who had been a surrogate father to Clover when she and her brother were growing up in a commune so many years ago, cleared his throat from across the room.

"I'm not messing with your recipe," Clover said, grinning. "Just wondering what you're making."

"Spring vegetable stew," Alvaro said. "And it would be nice if you two could start working and stop chatting." The cook, always on the salty side, softened his gaze when he looked at Megan. "Bonnie coming?"

Sometimes Bibi helped out in the kitchen. Alvaro and Bibi liked to pretend they couldn't stand the sight of one another, but in reality, they lived for their kitchen conflicts—and the chance to cook together.

"She'll be here before the lunch rush," Megan said, loving the fact that they even had a lunch rush. "Be nice to her. She's been a little melancholy lately."

"Alvaro is always nice—right, Alvaro?" Clover said, glaring at the older chef.

Alvaro let out a harrumph and moved on to the walk-in refrigerator, mumbling the whole way.

Megan shook her head slightly. "Some things never change."

"So...Bobby?" Clover said. "Can you give him a call? Maybe head him off before he goes to the farm?"

"Doing that now," Megan said, wondering why the chief hadn't just called her in the first place.

*   *   *

Megan reached King on the first try.

"Are you heading back to the farm?" King asked.

"Wasn't planning on it. Brian and Clay have things covered, so I figured I'd get some paperwork done here, at the café." Megan was in her tiny office, and her gaze fell on a letter that had been sent to the store. An advertisement addressed to Bibi. Absentmindedly, she picked it up. "What's going on, Bobby? Not like you to be coy."

"Oh, man. Hold on." Megan heard what sounded like a car horn before King returned to the line. "Just stay there. I'll come to the café."

"Bobby—"

"Trust me. I'll be there in twenty minutes, thirty tops." Then, more quietly, "Please."

Before King arrived, Megan had another visitor.

Clover popped her head into the office. "Can Merry come in? She says she needs to talk to you."

"I'm waiting for Bobby and trying to get this month's payroll squared away."

"She says it's important."

"Fine." With Merry Chance, it was always important. "Tell her I'll come out there. I could use some coffee."

Megan found Merry at a corner table in the café. She had a cup of tea in front of her and a Day Planner by her left elbow. Merry was one of those women whose age was impossible to discern. She could have been forty, she could have been sixty. Her closely-cropped hair—a new style for her—was bleached blond, and today the baby pink frames of the readers hanging at her throat matched the soft pink of her cardigan. She frowned when she saw Megan.

"I would have come to you," Merry said.

Megan placed a Washington Acres coffee mug on the table and slid onto the seat across from Merry. "I was tired of crunching numbers anyway. What's up?"

Merry glanced around before speaking. "Those women at my store yesterday. The three histrionic ones? One of them is missing."

"Still?"

Merry looked crestfallen. "So you knew already? They got a hold of you, then? They asked me your name."

"Yeah, I know. They came looking for me at the restaurant where Denver and I were having dinner last night." Megan took a sip of hot coffee, thinking. "So she's really still missing?" Which, Megan thought, is no doubt why Bobby King was headed over, too.

"You were the last to have seen her."

"I firmly doubt that. There were many people at the service."

Merry flashed a sly smile. "She never went inside. Melanie says she didn't show up."

"I don't know what to tell you, Merry. I dropped her off. I left. That was it. She was clearly upset—you witnessed that at the nursery. Maybe she ran off. Maybe she couldn't face Melanie, for whatever reason. I have enough going on without getting involved with their drama."

Merry's head swiveled, her attention on something across the room. "Looks like you're already caught up in it."

Megan turned around. Bobby King was in the store, standing by the counter, talking with Clover. He was looking at Megan, though.

"What did you want, Merry? Do you need help with something for the store?"

Merry shook her head. "I wanted to give you this." She pushed a piece of folded paper across the counter.

Megan picked it up, confused.

"You must have dropped it in the store. I saw...well, I thought perhaps it was important to you."

"Right. Thanks, Merry."

Merry reached out a hand and covered Megan's. She gave Megan an empathetic smile before vacating her seat for Bobby King, who was now hovering over the table.

"I'll be going now." Merry gave Megan's hand one last squeeze before leaving the café.

"What was that all about?" King asked, eyeing the paper in Megan's hand.

"Nothing. I was at Merry's store yesterday...anyway, want some coffee? Tea? A slice of Alvaro's strawberry rhubarb pie?"

"Can we go to your office?"

"My office over food? This must be serious."

"I'm in a rush."

"Okay, then," Megan said, noting King's uncharacteristic surliness. "I need the bathroom first, though."

While King headed for her office, Megan went into the staff bathroom, off the kitchen. She locked the door, leaned against the frame, and opened the papers Merry had given her. Two half sheets had been stapled together. The top one was a print-out from White Pages, with every Sawyer in Eastern Pennsylvania listed. The paper underneath was a printout of Megan's profile from a lawyer database. The name of her prior law firm was highlighted, and the number "three" had been printed underneath in heavy red pen.

Megan took a deep breath. These weren't papers that had

fallen from her purse or pocket. Someone had looked her up. Someone had researched her legal background and her address. The question was why?

"You look pale. Maybe *you* need some pie, Megan." King sat back in his chair and watched as Megan took a seat at the desk. He seemed to have some of his good humor back. "Feeling okay?"

"I'm fine. What's up that you couldn't discuss over the phone?"

Bobby studied her for a moment before responding. Finally he said, "The name Duke Masterman ring a bell?"

"The contractor?"

King steepled his fingers, pressing them together so that the tips turned white. "The contractor."

"What about him?"

"Did you ever use him?"

"He was supposed to work on the Marshall house but he...well, he reneged after getting a better deal from the von Tresslers. Why?"

"Reneged. Strong word. Sounds like you were angry at him for canceling on you."

"Who wouldn't be? Set me back months. By the time I found another contactor, it was too late in the season to do much outside. That's why we're just now finishing the project." Megan tilted her head. "What's with the questions about Duke? Seems to me you already know all this." She leaned forward, holding King's gaze. "Did something happen?"

"I don't know."

"You don't know?"

King sat back in his chair and turned his attention to his

fingernails. "I don't know."

"Spit it out, Bobby." Megan and the police chief had been through a lot together. She knew he trusted her as a friend and confidante. And in turn, she had great confidence in King. He was young, but he generally knew what he didn't know—a trait that was admirable in someone in a position of power.

"You know the von Tresslers? Melanie and her husband, David?"

"David who just passed away—yes."

"Well now the contractor is missing. Melanie is complaining. Says he left without finishing the job."

"Why is that your concern? Is she pressing charges?"

"Not yet, she's just making a lot of noise. Says he hasn't shown up for a week. I drove by his place this morning and no one is home."

"He lives alone."

"Right, and the neighbors say no pets. I've left messages for him and he hasn't responded."

"Have you searched his house?"

"No, and I don't plan to." King rubbed a paw of a hand against his temple. "I have no reason to suspect foul play, so there's only so much I can do."

Megan tapped a well-worn fingernail on the wooden desktop. "What do you want me to do?"

"I know you have work going on at the Marshall place. Keep your ear to the ground. See if you hear anything. I'd like to get Melanie and her mother off my back.

Megan mulled this over. "Did the von Tresslers pay Duke upfront?"

"That was my first question, too. I thought maybe they paid him, Duke got a better deal elsewhere, and he didn't feel like finishing the small projects left at the von Tressler mansion, so he dropped the project. It happens." King shrugged. "Only no one has seen him. At least no one I've spoken with." King's forehead puckered. "Duke has a reputation as a party boy. Could be as simple as that."

Megan agreed to keep her ear to the ground. "Did you get another call last night?"

King's eyes narrowed. "That's not enough?"

Megan explained the scene at Merry's flowers, the subsequent drive to the von Tresslers, and Claire's friends' claims that Claire never returned.

"Interesting. My admin said I had an urgent call this morning, but she sent it to one of my officers. I'll have to check in. You say this woman, Claire von Tressler, definitely went to the memorial?"

"I dropped her there myself."

King stood. "Well, we probably just have a lot of worked up people—death does that."

Megan thought of Bibi's strange words the night before. "Do you know for certain that Melanie is—was—David's wife?"

King looked confused. "Do I know for sure? It's not like I asked to see a marriage certificate. Why?"

"Because when I dropped Claire off, she claimed to be Claire von Tressler."

"She *said* she was David's wife?"

"I assumed she meant ex-wife. I had always assumed Melanie was his wife and the young man was their son, so I'm not really sure. It just seemed a curious thing to say."

King's look of confusion returned. "The von Tresslers don't have a son."

"The young man who looks like David. I've seen them together in town. Maybe a nephew or stepson." Megan shrugged. "Anyway, just wondering."

King grabbed the office's doorknob. "I think you're mistaken. I've been there twice now. No sign of any children. As far as I know, Melanie is the wife and their marriage didn't result in children." He paused there, his tall, bulky frame filling the doorway. "Why the sudden curiosity about the von Tresslers? They haven't exactly been a friendly addition to our community."

"No, they haven't. I guess it's just this woman, Claire. When I gave her a ride, she seemed truly distressed. Haunted, even. Frail." Megan shrugged, kneading the back of her neck with her hand. "I guess I'm just dwelling. If you haven't heard anything directly, she's probably turned up already."

"Let's hope so. We don't need more trouble in this town."

Megan watched King retreat into the café's kitchen, her mind still on Claire von Tressler. Wife, ex-wife—did it matter? Even beyond the family structure, she had a feeling there was more to the von Tresslers than met the eye.

Four

Friday brought rain showers and cooler temperatures. Summer in the Philadelphia region was typically warm, with temperatures in the upper eighties and a soup-like humidity that could drown the soul, but the region had been spared the worst of it—so far. Today's mild upper seventies was unusual, and Megan welcomed the fine mist of cool rain that was falling down on her ripening tomatoes. Tomorrow would be the first farmers market to which she would bring a hefty crop of tomatoes—always a big seller—and with this being the weekend before Monday's Fourth of July holiday, she was looking forward to the sales.

But before she could prepare for the market, she'd promised Bibi they'd walk through the new barn and discuss the grand opening, planned for the Fourth of July, so Megan headed toward the old Marshall property, thinking all the while about Monday's events.

Bibi would be hosting a free breadmaking class, Clay was giving a gardening workshop, and they were offering face painting by Clover as well as kids' games. There would be pizza from the Washington Acres' wood-fired oven and some of Alvaro's baked goods served throughout the day. Plus, they were hosting a mini farmers market with veggies and cut flowers from the farm.

Although the initial barn offerings would be an eight-week baking class taught by Bibi and a kitchen garden seminar Megan was teaching, they were hoping to increase the menu of classes over time, especially once the Marshall house was renovated. With the construction costs piling up, Megan wanted to get started. They could use the funds from classes to defray costs, and the barn's grand opening—although not so grand—would be a way to get locals to sign up.

The problem was time. Megan only had so much time to work on the farm, oversee the store and café, and get the Marshall place going. She needed help. She looked to her family and staff, but they were feeling it, too. So far, it had been a good growing season. While thankful for the farm's production, that meant Clay and Brian Porter, Megan's farm hand, were swamped. And with tourist season upon them, the café and store were busy, too, which meant Alvaro, Clover, and their part-time employee and family friend, Emily, were fully engaged. Bibi had more energy than most fifty-year-olds, but she could only do so much.

It was almost time to hire help, someone to live in the caretaker's apartment and be there when guests arrived. It wouldn't be a particularly stressful role—Megan would be overseeing the day-to-day, and with the farmhouse a few minutes' walk away, she'd always be around to assist. Nevertheless, Megan dreaded initiating the search. It was hard to find reliable people, and Megan had to make the time to train them properly. But as she made her way to the barn, she came to terms with the idea. What choice would she have once this property was up and running?

Her train of thought was derailed by Bibi, who was standing in front of the new barn holding a giant stainless-steel bowl and a pair of toast-shaped oven mitts. She waved at Megan before doing a little swirl-in-place to show off her skirt: a blue knee-length A-line made with a bread-print fabric.

Megan grinned. When Bibi embraced something, she went all in.

"Let's go, slowpoke," Bibi called.

Megan jogged the rest of the way to the barn. "Love your spirit." She hugged her grandmother, took the bowl from her grasp, and unlocked the barn entrance. "Ready?"

They both walked through the double door, into the new space.

Even now, thousands of dollars and many months later, the space moistened Megan's eyes. Unlike the old barn at Washington Acres, her original property, parts of which had been lovingly remade into a pizza kitchen by Clay and Porter, this space was airy and completely modern. Pine timber-framing gave a grand feeling to the entrance. Off to one side was a large room that had been slowly turned into a teaching kitchen. Four rows of counter-height tables, each capable of seating six, faced a simple wooden island with a cooktop in the center. Behind the island sat a row of cabinets with a triple sink, refrigerator, two dishwashers, and a microwave. The countertops were stainless steel; Clay and Porter had made the simple oak cabinets. The resulting look was clean and professional and, to Megan, a dream come true.

The other room was a classroom. Bookshelves lined one wall, white boards another. A long trestle table perched in the middle of the space. The rear of the room consisted of a bank of windows and a door to a small courtyard, which would eventually hold a *potager*—a small cutting garden with vegetables, herbs, fruits, and cutting flowers.

It was the perfect spot to teach and hold dinners. Once they could afford to get the place going.

Megan entered the kitchen area, put the bowl on the island, and smiled at her grandmother.

"Oh, Megan." Bibi walked across the room, touching the tables, and caressing the island. "When you came here, the farm was...well, it wasn't doing so well."

"Bibi—"

"Let me finish. Your dad is no businessman, bless him, and I'm too old to run a farm alone. Do you remember? The old barn was rotting. The storefront in town was boarded up. Even the house we live in was starting to show the wear and tear of neglect. And the Marshall house?" Bibi looked up at the soaring timber framing. "Everyone's nightmare neighbor—all abandoned darkness and shadows."

"Bibi—"

"You did this, Megan. You had a vision and you carried it through."

"It was our vision. And we had a lot of help."

Bibi simply smiled. She looked tiny and sweet standing there in her bread-themed clothes, but Megan knew there was iron will and a mother's fierceness under the adorable exterior. Which was why Bibi's words were bringing tears to her eyes and a tightness to her throat.

"Bibi, I can't—"

"You've created a legacy. The farm, this place, the café. You've done well." She touched Megan's hand. "Don't be afraid of what comes next. Denver, the farm, a life beyond what you have now. It can seem scary, Megan. Especially when you've been through so much in your short life."

Megan knew her grandmother was talking about her mother's abandonment at a young age, about the death of her husband, Mick. "Bibi—" But Megan's words were once again interrupted, this time by the sound of men shouting. Megan looked at her grandmother in alarm. "Do you hear that?"

Bibi tossed her potholders on the island. "It's coming from outside."

Megan ran through the barn and pulled open the main doors. From across the yard, she saw Ryan jogging from the back of the Marshall house and Porter and Clay running up from the farm. Ryan had his phone out and was tapping it as he moved. He stopped short when he spied Megan.

"Stay here," she said to Bibi, who was a few yards behind her. Her stomach tightened. Had one of the contractors fallen? Was it the animals?

Ryan motioned for Megan to accompany him to the back of the house. She sprinted, joined quickly by Porter and Clay.

It didn't take her long to see where the problem was. They were all peering into one of the ditches they'd started digging before the rains came. Megan couldn't quite bring herself to walk to the edge. A deer? A bear? Whatever was down there, it was bad. Ryan's eyes had taken on a hollow glaze, and his skin looked ashen.

Clay placed his hand on Megan's shoulder. She shook it off gently. It was her house, her duty to look. She edged closer.

The smell reached her first. Rotten and sweet at the same time, like a potato left too long in a dark closet. She looked down, bracing herself. She saw a clear plastic tarp, something twisted and white, one black high heel showed, the obscene press of distorted features beneath transparent plastic. But it was the flower bouquet that caught her attention. The mix of white lilies and orchids and irises—and one dried-up, blush-colored rose.

Claire von Tressler.

"My god," Megan said. She put her hand over her mouth. She felt faint, nauseous. Her eyes searched for Clay's, but he was behind her, supporting her.

"The police?" Porter asked.

"I called them a few minutes ago, when we found...this," Ryan said.

Megan was still staring into the abyss when she heard a high-pitched scream. "Grab her!" Someone yelled.

Megan turned just in time to see Bibi in Porter's arms, her face the color of bread dough, her mouth locked in a silent moan.

Not again, Megan thought.

"Not again," Clay whispered.

Five

It was well after nine that night before Bobby King called Megan.

"Want me to come there or do you want to come to the station?" he asked.

"You already took my statement—three times."

The police had been at the Marshall property for most of the afternoon and evening, and the back of the house was still cordoned off as a crime scene. Megan, Bibi, Clay, Porter, the contractors...they'd all been questioned. Local reporters had arrived and gone. Not much to say: as of the afternoon, the identification of the body hadn't been made public, and it remained unclear whether the woman had died on Megan's property or been transported there.

One thing *was* certain: foul play had been involved. No one trips and falls into a ditch while wrapped in clear plastic sheeting. The officers were silent, but the way the scene was being handled told Megan all she needed to know.

Murder.

"If this is an official police conversation, I'll come down, Bobby. But otherwise, I'd rather not leave Bibi, so I'd prefer you come here."

There was silence on the other end, during which Megan

heard a chair scraping the floor. "Give me a half hour. And I wouldn't say 'no' to a strong pot of coffee."

"Where's your grandmother?" King asked. He and Megan were sitting in the parlor, across from one another. Megan had brewed strong coffee, and King was nursing a cup, sipping from a "Smile, You're in Winsome" mug, a leftover from the days Megan's father had run a souvenir shop out of what was now the café.

"Bibi's sleeping. Her doctor ordered her a sedative. She refused it, of course—" Megan managed a weak smile, "—and made her own sedative instead."

"Chamomile tea with a shot of brandy?"

"Or two or three. Best kept secret in Winsome."

"Or not-so-secret." King ran a thick finger across the bottom of his mug, wiping away a few drops of water. He leaned back, into his seat. So many conversations had occurred here, Megan thought. So many emotional late-night chats. Was this to be another one?

"And Denver?" King asked.

"Handling an emergency. He's planning to come by afterwards, if it's not too late." In truth, Denver had tried to find someone to cover the emergency, insisting he be with her and Bibi. He'd been unsuccessful—summer is a busy month and large animal vets are hard to come by—but she didn't mind. They would catch up tomorrow. Tomorrow, once the dust settled, would be harder emotionally anyway. "So what's happening? Why was Claire von Tressler's body in my yard?"

King looked up over the rim of his mug, mid-sip. "Claire? The woman who disappeared from the memorial?"

"That's whose body it was, right? The shoes, the flowers—"

King shook his head. "No, Megan. That wasn't Claire von Tressler."

"Then who was it?"

"A woman named Penelope Greenleaf from Weston, Connecticut. Did you know her?"

"I'm confused...the flowers...I thought it was Claire."

"She's still MIA. It wasn't Claire. Penelope—or Penny as she was known—was a fifty-seven-year-old divorced piano teacher who was unlucky enough to be strangled in or near Winsome, Pennsylvania." King sat back in his chair. "Does the name mean anything to you?" He repeated it: "Penny Greenleaf."

"Her name means nothing. I recognized the shoes, the flowers. I'm thinking she was one of the women I met at Merry's." Megan picked up her own cup, put it down without drinking. Her mind flashed to the women at the restaurant, when they interrupted her dinner with Denver. "Did the victim have platinum-colored or red hair?"

"Platinum."

Megan nodded, a well of sadness building in her chest. Such a horrible thing, a life wasted. "She was there, at Merry's. Platinum-colored hair, well dressed. She was helping Claire. What about the other woman, the red head? Is she okay?"

"Olive Dunkel. Penelope's younger sister. She's fine—well, she's alive but understandably upset. She's the one who identified the body."

Megan considered this. "I don't understand. It was Claire they said was missing. How did this happen to Penny? If she went missing as well, why didn't Olive call the police? The women certainly made a fuss about Claire." She cocked her head. "Had a missing person report been made on Penny?"

"No. Olive claims that Penny had already left for Connecticut. She was due home for work—she taught piano at a private school in Weston—and Olive was to remain here to continue the search for Claire."

"And who is Claire? Another sister? A family friend?"

"Baby sister. There were four siblings, according to Olive. Penelope was the oldest. Claire is the baby."

"Quite an age gap between sisters."

"More than twenty years."

"And one is dead, one is missing."

King's smile was tight-lipped. "Yes. And one very much alive and extremely distraught."

"There's so much that doesn't make sense, like—" Sounds from above silenced Megan mid-sentence. Bibi heading to the bathroom. Megan placed a finger to her lips. Her grandmother needed rest more than Megan needed answers, and Megan thought it unlikely King had come with answers—only more questions.

King finished his coffee while they waited until Bibi's door had closed again. Sadie plodded down the stairs and laid by King's chair. He patted her head absentmindedly, a faraway look in his eyes.

King said, "Old house, thin walls."

"And thin ceilings." Megan stood up, stretched, and refilled King's mug. "Why were these sisters here to begin with? David von Tressler's memorial?"

"Based on what Olive said, yes—they were here for the memorial."

"Had they been in town long?"

"Just a few days."

Megan thought about her conversation with the youngest sister when she dropped her off at the memorial. "Still no sign of Claire?"

"Nothing. She's officially missing."

"Did you find out what the relationship between them was? Was Claire David's ex-wife?"

King smirked. "No. That's where things get...weird."

Megan waited, but when King didn't say more, she urged him with, "Bobby?"

"Megan, you do know I'm the one who is supposed to be asking the questions, right?"

Megan gave him a sheepish grin. "Ask away."

"Do you know why Penny's body was on your property?"

"I have no idea."

"You're sure you don't know Penny or Olive?"

"As I told you before, other than a brief encounter at Merry's, I had never seen them before."

King leaned forward. "You have no history with Claire von Tressler?"

Megan was starting to get alarmed by King's suddenly serious demeanor. "Bobby, no. And if I did, why would I hide it?" She thought of the paper Merry had found...the one with her law firm information. Irrelevant, she told herself. But was it?

King sat back. He drained his second mug of coffee. "I'm not trying to alarm you, Megan. The coroner believes Penny Greenleaf was strangled elsewhere and dumped on this property. Someone went to the trouble of bringing a dead body here. That concerns me."

"Obviously, that concerns me, too."

"And then we have the contractor, Duke."

"Did he ever show up?"

"No," King said. "No missing person report was ever filed, but given Penny's murder and his disappearance, we're looking into it."

"So one missing woman, one missing contractor—maybe, and one dead sister."

"That about sums it up." King worried the edge of his empty coffee cup with a calloused fingertip. "I want you to be careful. In fact, it might not be a bad time for you and Bonnie to live with Denver. Just temporarily."

"You know I can't leave. The animals, the crops. This is our busiest season." She swallowed, tasting the sourness of uncertainty. "We can't."

"Can't or won't?"

Silence hung between them until King finally stood and placed his cup in the sink. "You're a stubborn woman. Bonnie's even worse. Something stinks in Winsome, Megan, and I don't know where the smell is coming from, and until I do...well, there's a killer out there." He placed beefy hands on narrow hips. "I just want you and Bonnie to stay safe."

Megan tried hard not to react. He was right; the fact that Penny's body was found on their property *was* concerning. It made no sense. Why would the body of a relative stranger to Winsome be brought here? Coincidence? Or—the unspeakable, really—was someone from Winsome involved? Too many questions. No answers.

"Claire," Megan said softly. "You said she wasn't David's wife? You owe me that."

King sighed. "Claire von Tressler wasn't David's wife. Get this—that young woman was his *stepmother*."

Megan made her evening rounds with her Polish Tatra Sheepdog, Gunther, by her side. Sensing her angst, the massive dog adhered to her side, his sleek white body on high alert. The chickens were fine, the Pygmy goats, Dimples and Heidi, were nestled in their pen curled around one another like yin and yang. The farm was silent, lit only by a sliver of moon and a canopy of stars—and Megan's flashlight.

Tomorrow was the farmers market. She still intended to be there. She checked the Washington Acres barn and found it tightly locked and quiet. Up the hill, across the meadow, sat the Marshall property, dark except for a flood light on the back of the house that illuminated the yard and crime scene. Normally Megan would take a leisurely walk up there and check on the new barn and the construction site. Not tonight. No use asking for trouble, and with her nerves on edge...well, she was already seeing shadows everywhere.

Gunther growled, stopping Megan from moving farther. "What is it, boy?"

He crouched low and growled again.

Megan moved the flashlight to illuminate the fields near the barn. Nothing. But the light only flowed so far. Beyond that, darkness.

Megan glanced around her before moving backwards, toward the house. Gunther stayed in front of her, his attention beyond the field. Megan's jaw clenched, her shoulders squared. Had whoever killed Penny returned? Was it really that personal?

Movement caught the corner of Megan's eyes. She saw a white flash, and then Gunther relaxed. A bunny. Megan didn't let her guard down, though. Someone could have scared the rabbit, someone who was still lurking out there.

Megan called Gunther back to her side. Together they hiked back to the house, which Megan had locked while they were outside. She fumbled for the key and let herself in, grateful for Sadie's presence on the other side of the door.

They'd been through a lot at Washington Acres. She would not be scared in her own home. But she would not be stupid, either.

Tomorrow she'd talk to Clay about an alarm system for the

house. Bibi would balk, but that was okay. For some things, it really was better to ask forgiveness rather than permission.

The sound of a door closing woke Megan from a restless sleep. She sat up quickly and grabbed her phone off the bedside table. Sadie, who lay next to her on the bed, lifted her head, suddenly alert. Footsteps padded up the steps, and as they got closer, Sadie's posture changed. Her tail wagged against the mattress, her ears lowered. Megan smiled into her pillow, tension draining. No need for alarm. Familiar footsteps.

Her door opened. Megan could sense rather than see Denver across the room. A few minutes later, she felt his warm body slide into bed, next to hers.

"I hope you don't mind, Megs," he said. "I went home to shower and let out the dogs, but I was feeling lonely and worried."

"I don't mind at all," Megan whispered.

"Are ye okay?"

Megan turned to face him. She kissed his lips, then snuggled against his chest. "I am now."

Six

The farm looked friendlier in the light of day.

Megan, Clay, and Porter were gathering the last of the vegetables for the Winsome farmers market, which was being held down by the canal this year, on the town green. The town commission wanted to bring more people to Canal Street, with its sprinkling of shops and historically-accurate details. This was just fine by Megan. It meant that whatever veggies didn't sell could easily be carted up to the store for sale or for use by Alvaro at the café. But the space designated to each vendor by the canal was more limited, so Megan had to be thoughtful about which vegetables and fruits to load up on. Tomatoes were always a big seller. So were greens, and she still had plenty of spinach, kale, arugula, and Swiss chard. She'd bring hefty amounts of young onions and new potatoes as well—and a variety of other, less popular, offerings.

Clay was gently packing one of these lesser sellers—eggplant—into a crate. "So you're telling me that woman, Claire, was David von Tressler's stepmother?" Clay asked. He wiped sweat away from his eyes with the back of one well-muscled arm. In his late twenties, Clay looked like a sinewy Jake Gyllenhaal. When he wasn't farming, he was studying engineering—or spending time with his maybe girlfriend, Emily.

Porter perked up. "Wasn't David in his seventies?"

"Sixty-two," Megan said, "at least that's what his obituary says. He was sixty-two, and based on my interaction with Claire, she's in her early- to mid-thirties."

"David's father is her husband?" Porter asked. He was counting heads of Romaine lettuce and logging the numbers on a piece of paper. "Is or was?"

"*Was.* Apparently, the late Martin von Tressler remarried after his second wife died. At the time, Claire was in her late twenties and Martin was eighty-one. He died a few years later."

"To put in in perspective," Porter said, "that's like your grandmother marrying Clay."

Megan let that sink in. "I suppose so."

"Is she loaded now?" Porter asked. "That's why she married the dude, right? Money."

Megan did a quick stretch before washing her hands in the barn sink. "I didn't find much online, but I didn't search long. The father—Martin—owned a chain of furniture stores across the Northeast. He parleyed his money into investments, and eventually von Tressler Investments was born. The furniture stores and the family's old mansion are still intact in the city. Best I can tell, David worked for his dad's company—the parent investment company—until Martin's death."

"His dad's company—or his company?" Clay asked. "Didn't David inherit the business?"

Megan raised a pointer finger. "Good question. I don't know. I also don't know whether he had siblings. Normally wills are in the public domain once they've been through probate. Martin didn't die long ago, though, and there could be contention around the terms of the will. I couldn't find it online."

"I'm sure you'll figure it out," Porter said.

Clay laughed. "The detective's in the house."

Megan surveyed the barn, ignoring their playful teasing. Crates of tomatoes sat next to boxes of vegetables and cut flowers. Everything needed to be loaded into the truck. The market started in two hours, so they had to get going so they could set up in time.

"Are you sure want to go?" Clay asked, suddenly serious. "Porter and I can handle it."

"I could use the distraction."

Clay opened the door and glanced outside. "At least the weather's holding up. Should be a nice day."

"Nice as in ninety degrees and not raining?" Porter asked.

Clay said, "Nice as in mild and not raining."

Megan smiled. "I'll take that."

The trio silently loaded the back of Megan's truck with goods for the market. Clay filled his SUV, too, and offered to take Porter with him. Gunther galloped from across the yard and stood in front of Megan's vehicle, begging to go.

"Why don't you take him?" Clay said.

Megan shook her head. Bibi would be here. "I'd rather he stay with my grandmother."

Clay's nod was of the solemn variety. "Makes sense." He glanced sideways at Megan after Porter had gotten into the car. "People are talking, Megan. You must know that. The body was found here, after all. So few details have been released."

It was a small town. Plus, Merry loved to talk—and her shop was arguably where it all started. Add a body on her property, and it was a recipe for gossip galore. "I figured."

"Nothing bad...but they're curious. You might find it weird at the market."

"I have to face it one way or another—at the market or at the café."

He nodded again. "Are you still doing the Fourth grand

opening?"

Megan looked in the direction of the Marshall house. She couldn't see the police tape, but she knew it was there. "I don't see how I can."

"We could postpone it until the following weekend."

Megan studied her farm manager with warmth in her eyes. He was such a kind soul, always seeing the best in people. "I don't think so, Clay. I want folks to come to the barn because they want to learn about sustainable living, not because they want to gawk at a crime scene." She smiled, but it didn't reach her eyes. "We'll get through this, but I want to postpone the barn opening indefinitely. Until...until things have died down."

She immediately realized her poor choice of words and blushed. If Clay noticed, he didn't let on. He jogged ahead to his SUV. Megan watched him pull out of the driveway before patting Gunther one more time and making her own way off the property, toward the center of Winsome.

The farmers market was a bustling affair. The usual Winsome suspects were manning booths—local farmers, craftspeople, bakers, chefs, and artists displaying a wide range of products and prepared foods. The atmosphere was jovial, the weather sunny and mild, the scents of doughnuts and caramel corn fighting it out with Joe Riley's smoked brisket. Megan and Clay arranged their two tables, neatly stacking their offerings in a cornucopia of colors and shapes. Porter was reorganizing the truck bed so they could easily reach extra produce if they needed it, and he grinned broadly at Megan from the back end of the tent.

"Should be a good day."

Megan returned the smile. "Hope so. We could use one."

Clay wiped his hands with a clean cloth. "Going to get some coffee. Back in five. Want some?"

Megan shook her head. "No thanks. I drank a pot all by myself this morning."

Megan was putting the final touches on a bucket full of flower bouquets when she felt a presence standing behind her. She turned slowly, smiling, expecting it to be Denver, who'd promised to try to end appointments early and join her for lunch at the market. Instead she was met with a mop of red hair, eyes so heavily shadowed they looked bruised.

"Olive," Megan said. "I'm so sorry about your sister."

Olive Dunkel was a round woman who looked to be in her early- to mid-fifties. Red hair contrasted with black eyebrows and clashed with the pink tunic she wore over black capri pants. She raked long red nails through her hair and gave Megan a ghost of a smile.

"I'm sure you're sorry," she said.

"I am. What happened...it was awful and needless."

"And it will happen again soon if we don't do something about it." She clawed at Megan's arm with surprising strength. "Where did you leave Claire? Please. You have to tell me. She's in danger, too."

"I left her at the memorial."

"She never arrived there. I know she had you take her somewhere else, somewhere secret. I'm sure she made you promise not to tell, but now's not the time for—"

Clay arrived back at the tent with coffee in one hand and a pumpkin muffin in the other. He raised his eyebrows behind Olive's back.

"Olive, since Clay is back, why don't we go talk somewhere else?" The last thing Megan wanted was the Winsome townspeople to overhear Olive talking about her sister's death.

More fuel for the gossip fire. "Clay, will you be okay here with Porter?"

"Sure. Don't stray too far."

His words were a reminder that he would be looking out for her, and Megan nodded her gratitude. She led Olive to the far end of the market, where "seats" consisting of hay bales and a few picnic tables served as a makeshift cafeteria. She and Olive sat across from one another at the end of an empty table.

Mentally noting the woman's disheveled appearance and sickly skin color, Megan asked, "Can I get you some coffee? Soup? Maybe a muffin?"

"Just Claire."

"Look, Olive, I don't know where your sister is. I took her to the von Tressler house and dropped her off." Megan kept her voice low but her tone stern. She knew this woman must be distraught, but she also knew there was more going on than she could discern. She didn't know or trust Olive Dunkel or anyone related to the von Tresslers, and the body that had turned up on her property told her that distrust was called for.

Olive stretched her hands out in front of her, then tightened them into fists. Her hands were creamy white, unsullied by callouses or rough patches of skin, but they were shaking. "Claire is...special. You were at the florist the day of the memorial. You saw how upset Claire got. She's not a stable person. She's had a lot of tragedy in her life, a lot of loss. She's only thirty-one."

At the look of surprise that crossed Megan's features, she said, "Penny, our brother, and I were the planned-for children. Claire was a surprise. She's the baby, and as the baby she was spoiled by everyone. It was as though she had three mothers— my mother, Penny, and me. Our father died when Claire was a kid."

"I'm sorry."

Olive dabbed at her eye with the back of a knuckle. "I loved Penny dearly. She was my best friend. But Claire? She never knew our father like we did. He was a good man, stable and kind and hard working. By the time she was a teen, our mother was having health issues. Penny and I raised her. She's like a daughter, and I want her found." She slammed her hand down on the table, then winced at the impact.

Megan glanced at the Washington Acres tent. Clay was handling a small line of customers while Porter refreshed the piles of cucumbers and tomatoes. They seemed to be fine.

Softly, Megan said, "Olive, why would someone want to hurt Penny?"

"I have no idea." Olive sniffled. "She had no enemies. Everyone loved her. She was a nice person, a teacher. Good with kids."

"Do you think what happened is related to Claire's disappearance?"

"In my heart? Yes. That's why I think Claire's in danger." Olive's voice began to escalate in pitch and volume. "She must have known something was up. That's why she asked you to take her somewhere else. She was trying to protect us, so she swore you to secrecy—"

Megan held up a hand. "If we're going to get to the bottom of this, you need to stop accusing me of that. I dropped her off at the memorial. I'm not lying, I'm not hiding anything."

Olive glanced down at her hands, flexed her fingers. "I'm sorry."

"You're distraught," Megan said. "I understand that. What makes you think Claire asked me to drive her somewhere other than the memorial? She seemed anxious to attend. What would cause her to change her mind?"

"She's an impulsive girl."

"She's a thirty-one-year-old woman."

"Who has made bad choices before." Olive once again grasped Megan's arm. Megan pulled away, and Olive raked fingernails along the outside of her purse, kneading it nervously. "Do you know who my sister is? She is—was—David's stepmother. *Stepmother*, for god's sake. My thirty-one-year-old sister married an octogenarian and then proceeded to fall in love—" Olive clapped a hand over her own mouth. "She's made bad choices."

"She told me her last name was von Tressler. I thought maybe she and David had been married."

"Even David would have been too old for her. My sister is impulsive and emotional and, yes, often childish and manipulative. I know she didn't want to go to that memorial. She never wanted to go. We made her go. We made her go!" Olive clutched her bag to her chest. She looked suddenly weary, as though the fire that had propelled her to the market to question Megan had left her hollow and exhausted.

"Why?" Megan asked softly. "Why was it so important to you that she go?"

"We said she needed closure. She had buried David's father, now she would bury the son. We said she needed to move on with her life." Olive shook her head. "We said a lot of convincing things."

"They weren't the real reasons?"

Olive flashed a sardonic smile. "Do you know how much the von Tressler business is worth?"

"No idea."

"Tens of millions. With David gone, his heir stands to inherit a fortune. My sister needed to show up at that service with her head held high. She was Martin's wife, the von Tressler rightful heir." A hardness returned to Olive's eyes, a hardness, Megan thought, that gave another perspective on who this woman was. "She deserves his fortune."

"Wouldn't she have received it already?"

"There are complications. Messy family stuff." She threw her hands up in the air. "Oh, it doesn't matter now. None of it matters." Olive moved back, away from the table. "I don't know where to go from here. Penny gone, Claire missing. I feel helpless, and the police have been useless."

"They're trying to get to the bottom of this, just like you are. Just like I am."

Olive stood up awkwardly from the picnic table bench. She glowered at Megan with a mixture of contempt and frustration. "I know you insist that you took Claire to that memorial, but no one saw her there. Either everyone is lying, or you are." Her lips twisted into a sneer. "And then my sister's body was found on your farm. Forgive me if I don't trust you."

"Why would I want to hurt either of your sisters, Olive? Please, be rational and think about that. While you're busy blaming me, someone else may be getting away with a monstrous crime."

Olive took a deep breath. She looked ready to respond, but clutched her purse to her chest and walked away instead, leaving Megan on the bench alone.

"What the hell was that all about, Megs? We were watching ye from across the market and it looked like that woman was going a bit mental." Denver had, indeed, shortened his workday and now stood in front of Megan looking deliciously unkempt in jeans and a tight black t-shirt, his auburn hair pushed back from his face in unruly waves. "Clay said you were okay, so we didn't interrupt."

Olive had left as quickly as she'd come, disappearing beyond the crowd that was congregating around a makeshift stage, near the parking area. Megan gave Denver a quick rundown on their conversation.

"The oddest thing," Megan said, "were the emotional transitions. One second she was angry at me, then she was sad, then she was enraged." Megan told him what she'd said at the end. "She's so fixated on me that she's not even considering a bigger picture."

"I'm sorry she upset you, Megs," Denver said. "She's just bereft."

"That's what I keep telling myself."

A family of five stopped by the table, and while the adults made their selection, Megan watched their two youngest, identical twin girls about four years old, argue over a stuffed dinosaur. A nearly identical dinosaur hung from the backpack of the more vocal twin.

"Give it to me!" One twin said, trying to grab the dinosaur from the other twin.

Denver squatted down so that he was eye level with the girls. "What are ye fighting about, little lassies? Don't ye know what kind of a dinosaur ye have there?"

The girls stopped fighting and regarded him, mesmerized. He was using the voice he saved for scared animals and their humans, soft and soothing, with his Scottish accent turned up for full effect.

"Ah, I didn't think ye knew. That there is a Stegosaurus. The Stegosaurus liked its salads. Did ye know that?"

Two little brunette head shakes.

"And this one here," he unclipped the other dinosaur from its ring on the backpack of the more assertive twin, "that is a

Brachiosaurus. The biggest plant-eating dinosaur."

As soon as he said 'biggest,' the more vocal twin grabbed the stuffed animal gently from his hand. "Mine."

The other sister looked ready to protest before hugging her animal to her chest.

"Ye both have fine dinosaurs, so that's good."

The girls' mother came over and graced Denver with a warm smile. "Once they get started, it's hard to get them to stop. They won't separate, but they won't stop fighting." She glanced at Megan. "Your husband is good with kids. Are you a teacher?"

When Denver shook his head, she said, "Pediatrician?"

"Veterinarian."

The mother laughed. "Well, that explains it." She held up a giant bag of tomatoes. "We'd better move on. Thanks again."

When the family was out of earshot, Megan echoed the woman's compliments. "How did you know what kind of dinosaurs they were? They just looked like stuffed lumps to me."

"I made it up."

"It satisfied them."

"It satisfied the one who needed to be satisfied. The louder girl was the alpha. She needed to feel like her toy was better, or she needed to get what she thought was the better toy. Some people are like that."

Megan laughed. "So you told her that her dinosaur was the biggest plant eater out there so she'd leave her sister's toy alone."

"Didn't know you had such a smart guy?"

"Smart husband, apparently." As soon as the words were out of her mouth, Megan regretted them. The happy look on Denver's face evaporated. The subject of marriage—the topic of a future beyond what they shared now—had become taboo. He wanted more. Megan knew that. The problem was, she didn't know what she wanted. More specifically, she was afraid that if she wanted more, she would lose what she had now.

"Lunch?" Megan said in an effort to lighten the now-sullied mood.

"It's only 10:12."

"Brunch, then. My treat."

Megan led the way to the food trucks, but her mind was lingering on something Denver had said. The alpha sister going after what she wanted. Megan had no sisters, but she wondered whether that was often the case between siblings—that one sibling had to be in charge. If so, which sister was—or had been—the alpha in Claire's family? The von Tresslers were rich. Was Claire as impulsive and childlike as Olive had suggested? Or had someone else in her family been pulling her strings to get to the von Tressler fortune?

Seven

For the first time that summer, Megan canceled the pizza farm kitchen. The summer before, a portion of the barn at Washington Acres had been turned onto a wood-fired pizza oven and restaurant. Open only on the weekends, and with limited picnic table-style seating, it quickly became a favorite Saturday night destination. Megan, Clay, and the rest of the farm team served up pizzas made with local cheeses, meats, and vegetables. But not this Saturday. For the same reason Megan was delaying the opening of the Marshall property, she'd decided to close the pizza farm for a few weeks. She wanted people to come to the farm to enjoy the food and camaraderie, not to gawk at a crime scene.

Bibi didn't agree.

"Let them gawk. We didn't do anything wrong. It's not your fault Bobby and his people can't catch whoever did that to the woman." Bibi was making bread, kneading the dough in long, firm strokes. "If I've learned anything in my eighty-plus years on God's gorgeous green earth, it's that people will talk no matter what. Who cares?"

"I'd rather let the talk die down."

Bibi wiped a hand across the bridge of her nose, painting a band of flour under her eye. "Suit yourself." She nodded her head toward the parlor. "You have a visitor."

Megan raised arched eyebrows. "Really?" After the farmers market, she had gone to the café to call everyone on tonight's reservation list. Porter and Clay returned to the farm, and Megan hadn't seen any cars in the driveway other than theirs.

"Who's here?"

"Porter. The poor boy looks exhausted and way too skinny, so I set him up in front of the television with a nice piece of pie and some coffee. You need to pay him more." She wagged a flour-covered finger at her. "That's why you shouldn't be canceling pizza night. That's money in the bank, Megan. Money for the farm. Money for paying Brian Porter."

Megan backed out of the kitchen. Her grandmother was clearly feeling ornery today. "Okay, Bibi," she said as she left.

She found her farm hand reclining in Bibi's chair, watching baseball on television. An empty plate and a half-empty cup sat on the table beside him, along with a crumpled-up napkin, a pair of work gloves, and a large, flat brown envelope. Porter frowned when he saw Megan.

"Don't look so excited to see me."

"I'd be more excited under different circumstances."

Megan sat on the couch across from Porter and regarded her employee. She'd given him a job at Denver's urging a few years ago. A former veteran, PTSD survivor, and recovering alcoholic, Porter had seen more of the world than most people twice his age—and it showed. Tall and lanky, he was a strong slip of a man, heavily tattooed and fiercely private. Megan respected him. He worked hard, showed sound judgment, and he was kind to the animals. But today he looked especially somber, and that had her worried.

"What could have changed between the market and now, Brian? You seemed fine then."

Porter gave her an ironic smile. They both knew a lot could

change in an instant.

Porter held out the envelope. "I was checking the barn on the old Marshall place. Just walking around after the market, making sure everything is buttoned up, and I ran into Ryan. He and his crew are working inside the house now, but earlier they found this."

Megan accepted the envelope. Slowly, carefully, she undid the metal clasp.

Porter handed her the gloves. "Use these."

The gloves were too big, but she slipped them on anyway. Inside the envelope was a folded, muddied copy of her late husband's obituary. Printed on plain white paper, its edges were creased in a number of places, as though it had been folded and unfolded many times.

Megan looked up at Porter. "I don't understand. Where did Ryan find this?"

"Near the Marshall house."

"Near as in...?"

"Behind the house."

Megan stood up. "You mean by the crime scene?"

"I take it you didn't drop it?" When Megan shook her head, Porter's chiseled jaw tightened. "Yes—kind of. I asked Ryan to show me where they'd found it. It was next to the Bilco doors."

As in the doors that led into the basement. "It could have been there for ages."

"Ryan said they walk through that area all the time. Some of his crew were working in the basement, and that's their main way in and out."

"Had it been left in a way that was obvious? Like someone wanted us to find it?"

Porter shrugged his shoulders. "You'll have to ask Ryan. I don't know which of his men found it. I wish they hadn't touched it—it could be evidence." He pointed to a corner of the paper. "Some of that mud has a reddish tint."

"Blood?"

"Maybe."

Megan thanked him. She wished they hadn't touched it as well. "Why did you assume someone left it there? It could have been me—I could have dropped it by the house."

Porter was quiet for a moment. When he responded, his voice had a husky, emotional quality that Megan found unsettling. "I have a bad feeling, Megan. I figured you wouldn't be walking around with this in your pocket, and the fact that the woman's body was found on your property?" Porter's eyes narrowed. "I think somehow you're connected to all of this."

Megan reclosed the envelope. She thanked Porter again and left for the kitchen. She was part way down the hallway when she felt a hand on her shoulder.

"I'm staying here," Porter said.

"We'll be fine, Brian."

He shook his head. "I've never crossed you, Megan. When you and Bonnie have said you'll be fine in the past, I took you at your word—and you *were* fine. But this is different." He pointed to the envelope. "I have a soldier's gut feeling, and it's not a good one. That barn up on the old Marshall property is clean and new. Sarge can stay with Denver, and I'll camp there for a while."

"Brian—" Megan started. She appreciated his thoughtfulness, but they would be fine. She was looking into an alarm system, and they had the dogs.

"It's as much for me as for you. We all put a lot into this place. The farm. The Marshall property. Let me stay."

Megan searched the younger man's eyes for a sign that this was all bravado, but what she witnessed was sheer concern. She nodded. "Stay at the house."

Porter laughed. He had old-soul eyes, but his smile spoke of youth and vigor. "I'm not much of an inside guy."

"Then at least let Sarge stay here." Sarge was Porter's rescued German Shepherd. The dog had as many psychological battle wounds as Porter, and they had long ago saved one another. The barn was off limits to animals because of the kitchen—the Commonwealth's rules—but Sarge and Gunther got along, and Sadie got along with everyone.

"He'd like that."

Megan half smiled. "I'll see you later, then."

"Wait, where are you going with that?" Porter asked, referring to the envelope.

Megan shook the envelope. "This? Taking it with me. Time to chat with Bobby King."

After trying the local police department, Megan decided to bypass official channels and talk to the man at his home. She called his cell first, and a surprised King told her to come over. Clover was at the café, but he was watching baseball and would be there for another two hours.

Bobby King and Clover Hand lived together across town in a modest apartment owned by King's parents. King met Megan at the door wearing sweatpants, a t-shirt, and a Phillies baseball cap. He invited her inside with a sweep of his muscular arm and led Megan into a lushly decorated living room. A couch took center stage, its surface covered with what looked like jewel-toned sari fabrics sewed into a richly-colored patchwork. On the wood floor, surrounding a low coffee table, were large cushions covered in a similar material. An ornate silver hookah had been placed on an antique teacart in the corner of the room next to stacks of travel books and framed photos of Clover and King. An old navy blue recliner positioned next to the couch, it's covering decidedly frumpy and worn, was the sole decorative outlier.

King plopped down on the recliner and motioned for Megan to have a seat on the couch.

"Very hers and his," Megan said with a smile. *Very Clover* is what she was thinking.

King laughed. "Clover has very specific taste, as you know. She allowed me to keep this chair. It's my equivalent of a man cave. A tiny island of comfort in a sea of eclectic artistry and eco-travel keepsakes." King glanced at the envelope in Megan's hand, and his expression darkened. "But you're not here to talk about interior design, are you?"

"I'm afraid not." Megan unclasped the envelop. After donning a pair of gloves, she pulled the obituary out of its holder and placed it on the coffee table. "Ryan, my contractor, found this today."

King stared at the paper. "It's not something you might have dropped?" he asked softly.

"No, Bobby. I don't carry a copy of Mick's obituary with me. It's not Bibi's either."

"Where did Ryan find it?"

"Near the Marshall house."

"Near the crime scene?"

"Yes." Megan reached into her purse. "There's more." She slid the print-out from the legal database across the table to him. He picked it up.

"I don't understand, Megan. This is just information about you when you used to work for the law firm. Was this with Mick's...with the other thing?"

"No. The print-out about me was found at Merry's store the day Claire and her sisters picked up flowers for the memorial."

"Why didn't you tell me before?"

"I didn't think it was important."

King's eyes lit up with understanding. "The obituary, the print-out—you think Penny's body on your property is no coincidence."

Megan knew it sounded flimsy, but why else would these documents be floating around? "Look," she said, "I'm just sharing what we found. If Penny's body hadn't turned up on my property, I wouldn't be here. But it did. Information about me— information about a life I haven't led in years—was found at Merry's the same day Penny happened to be there, and now Mick's obituary. Don't you think it's awfully coincidental?"

"You're sure none of this belongs to Bonnie?"

"I'm certain."

"Maybe someone in town wants to meet you, Megan. Maybe they're researching you for an article or a podcast. Small town girl makes it big before returning to her roots, something like that." He shrugged. "It could be as simple as someone doing their homework."

Megan sat back against the couch. It smelled of patchouli and lavender, comforting scents that gave her no comfort. "Or maybe someone is stalking me or my family."

"We searched that whole property. If this had fallen out of the killer's belongings, don't you think we would have found it before now?"

Megan had thought of that. "It's not necessarily something the killer had, Bobby. What if someone dropped it there to intimidate. Someone who would know we'd be on edge and wanted to drive home the point that we're not safe." She met King's gaze. "You said it yourself the night you urged me to call a security company."

"Everything should be considered, but this seems tenuous.

Nevertheless, Penelope Greenleaf *was* found on your property."
King chewed on his bottom lip. "I just don't know."

"Take a harder look at it."

Megan handed him her gloves, and he slipped them on. He peered at the paper, holding it close to his face. "This mud—"

"Has a reddish coloring, I know. It's not the red of our clay soil."

King nodded. "You think it's blood? We'll take this and have it analyzed. In the meantime, if you see or hear anything—*anything*—call me. Please."

"Was there blood on Penny's body?"

"She'd been strangled, that was the official cause of death, but there had been a struggle. Whoever killed her had subdued her, and whatever blood we found was Penny's." King nodded toward the obituary, now tucked into its envelop. "You're thinking that's Penny's blood?"

Megan nodded.

King took an audible breath. He stood up stiffly and walked to the kitchen. He placed the envelope on the counter before opening the refrigerator. "Soda? Beer?"

"No thanks. I need to get back to the farm."

"I was hoping you could stay a few more minutes. Hold on a sec." He returned a moment later with a Pepsi and a bag of chips in his hand. "Sure you don't want anything?"

"I'm fine."

King nodded. He seemed to be searching for a way to say something. Finally, "That woman, Claire, she hasn't turned up."

"I know. Her sister Olive confronted me at the farmers market this morning."

"Confronted you how?" King took a swig of soda before placing the can on a coaster on the coffee table. "Was she belligerent?"

"More like erratic. Emotional one minute, cold the next."

"She did just lose her sister."

"And another one is missing," Megan said. "Reasons to be abrasive and emotional. Why would you think she'd been belligerent?"

"Because she keeps telling us to check you out, that you were the last one to have seen her sister."

"And I keep telling her that I dropped Claire off at the von Tressler house."

King frowned. "It's been several days since anyone has seen Claire. Right now, we have no evidence of foul play, but her disappearance is suspect given her sister's death."

"Any leads on what happened to Penny?" Megan knew she was treading on fragile ground. King often looked to her for help, but he was a public servant—and a good one—and he would guard information if he had to, even from her. She didn't want to put him in a compromising position.

"Nothing so far. My people have talked to Melanie and her staff. We interviewed others who may have seen or talked with Penny before her death, including family members. Nothing concrete—yet."

"Do you think it could have been random, Bobby? Wrong place, wrong time sort of thing?"

King shook his head. "No signs of rape or robbery. Her car was found where she was staying, so we believe whoever killed her knew her schedule or had been following her."

Making it less likely it was a random killing, Megan thought. "How about some of the guests who were in from out of town for the memorial?"

"We talked with those we could track down based on the registry. It was helpful that Merry showed up."

Megan's eyes widened in amusement. "So she did go? She

was threatening to attend."

"Yes, she went, although she was late." King's scrunched up scowl told Megan exactly what he thought about Merry attending the memorial reception. "She very definitely did not see Claire there, but she did see Penny. Penny and Olive went to pay their respects and pick up their sister, only as we both know, Claire never showed up."

"So Penny was at the memorial—and then what? She left to go to which hotel?"

"She and her sister stayed overnight at the Bucks County Inn."

Megan remembered that inn well; it was a local place, convenient to Winsome, where Denver's friends had stayed during the tragedy last summer. "I'm sure the proprietor remembers her."

King nodded. "We spoke to her. Says nothing odd happened. Penny got to her room the evening of the memorial, she and her sister went to bed in separate but neighboring rooms, she rose the next morning to leave for home."

"And then she was murdered."

King lowered his head. "And then she was murdered."

"And her body placed on my property."

King didn't respond to the last statement. Instead he asked, "Did Olive say anything else that could be helpful?"

Megan replayed their conversation in her head. "She talked about the von Tressler fortune and the fact that Claire deserved the inheritance from Martin. I tried to find the will but couldn't. Have you seen it?"

King shook his head. "It's one of the things we're working on."

"Seems like Claire should have inherited already."

"Older man marries younger woman. Maybe there was a

prenup, and the son got everything."

"Maybe." Megan wasn't convinced. "And now that David's dead, perhaps things get even messier."

King said, "I thought David was a partner in the business. Wouldn't his half go to Melanie?"

"That's what I would think, too, but clearly there was some bad blood over von Tressler Senior's death." Megan rubbed her forehead, forcing herself to remember the details of the conversation with Olive. "Olive made it sound as though Claire is flighty and unstable. Our whole conversation made me wonder who was pulling the strings in the family. Olive waffled between caring older sister and drill sergeant."

"You think someone is controlling Claire? Someone in her family?"

"I got the distinct feeling that she's being pushed to fight for a share of the von Tressler family fortune."

"Estate dispute, huh?"

"A prime motive for murder." Megan decided to give voice to the thing that had been bothering her. "There's something else, Bobby. When I first saw the sisters at Merry's, Claire was upset, distraught even. I had the distinct sense that she was mourning someone very close to her. *Very* close."

"You think Claire and David were having an affair?"

"Penny stopped short of saying so, but I think it's a possibility we can't ignore."

"Another motive for murder."

"But Penny's murder?"

King looked away, chewing at his lip again. "One sister dead, the other missing. Definitely things we need to follow up on. If there's a connection, if Penny's death is related to a fight over money, how do you fit in?"

Megan stared at the print-out of her short legal career,

which still sat on the coffee table next to King's drink. "I have no idea, Bobby. None at all." She looked up. "But I'd really like to find out."

Eight

Megan drove to the café, all the while thinking about her conversation with King. She knew he would be all over this, but she couldn't help feeling that he wasn't taking the connection to her or her family seriously. Maybe she was nuts. But maybe, just maybe, she wasn't. The fact that Penny's body had been found at Washington Acres left her feeling vulnerable. Worse, it left her feeling like Bibi was vulnerable. She needed to help King, whether he wanted her help or not.

She decided to start with the beginning: the von Tresslers. She had only half paid attention to the rumors before now because she didn't really care—and they didn't affect her. First, she needed to make absolutely certain the obituary and legal database print out didn't belong to her grandmother.

She found Bibi in the back of the kitchen, washing knives in hot, soapy water in the café's three-basin sink. She gave her grandmother a hug.

"Your goats escaped again," Bibi said. "I had to send Porter in the woods after them."

"How come when they do something mischievous, they're my goats?" Megan asked. She could tell from Bibi's tone that the goats were fine—now, at least.

"They're always your goats. They just happen to like me better." Bibi flashed a cheeky smile.

"That's because you feed them things they're not supposed to have."

Bibi dismissed the accusation with a wave of one soapy hand. "Why are you here? I thought you were planting more lettuce this afternoon, at least that's what Porter told me."

Megan asked her grandmother if she'd misplaced anything lately. "Paperwork? Maybe a copy of Mick's obituary?"

"No. Why?"

"No reason." Megan thanked her grandmother and was about to head to the dining area to find Clover when she heard her grandmother clear her throat—always a precursor to a lecture.

"You're doing it again," Bibi said.

"Doing what?"

"Trying to protect me. Stop it. What's going on?"

Reluctantly, Megan told Bibi about the two papers. "Bobby's submitting the obituary for tests. Ryan's crew touched it, but there's a reddish stain that could be blood."

Bibi's face was stony-still. "That explains Porter."

"What do you mean?"

"I saw him putting a sleeping bag and stuff in the new barn. I was wondering." Bibi was drying a chef's knife on a white towel. She stopped drying. "Please stop hiding things. The alarm system company called you back. I do not want an alarm system—two dogs are enough of an alarm." She lowered her voice. "I know security is an issue after what happened, and I can tell you're worried, Megan. We're a team. You need to be able to tell me when you're worried. I can help."

Eyeing the knife, which was bouncing up and down in Bibi's hand in Megan's direction, Megan said, "Maybe we can start with you putting down the knife."

Bibi looked down at her hand, murmured "oh," and placed

the knife on the chopping block alongside a pile of herbs. "Do you hear me, Megan?" Her voice kinder, she said, "We've been through a lot. I know you worry about me, but I'm a lot tougher than you give me credit for."

"Oh, I know you're tough, Bibi. Why do you think I asked you to put the knife down?"

"I'm not kidding."

Megan nodded. "I know, and I'm sorry. I'm not kidding, either. I know how strong you are. But aside from Denver...well, you're my family."

"You have Aunt Sarah, and your mother."

Megan's relationships with her grandfather's sister Sarah and Megan's estranged mother had improved over the past years, but when Megan thought of family, she thought of Bibi. "Not the same and you know it."

Bibi began chopping herbs—chives and mint and cilantro—with deft strokes. "Tell me about the flowers," she said.

"The flowers?"

"You thought the woman found on the Marshall property was Claire von Tressler because of the flowers, right?"

"Right. Flowers and designer shoes."

"When you dropped Claire off, did she have the flowers with her?"

The flowers! Megan threw her head back, exasperated with herself. "The flowers. Of course. She did have them in the car, so she must have taken them with her. I was in such a hurry, I wasn't really paying attention."

"And then they ended up with the woman who was murdered."

"Penny—Penelope Greenleaf."

"Penny." Bibi stopped what she was doing before whamming down on a pile of chives with a strong chop.

"Greenleaf."

"Recognize the name?"

"I don't think so. But the fact remains: if Claire took those flowers out of your truck, somewhere between then and Friday when her body was found, someone else got a hold of those flowers."

"Likely the same someone who killed Penny."

Bibi used a pastry cutter to sweep up the chopped herbs and place them into a stainless-steel bowl. "Old man!" she yelled to Alvaro. "Here are the herbs you were whining about."

"Always nagging," Alvaro said. No one was fooled by his feigned grouchiness, though—least of all Megan. "Took you long enough." Something fragrant was bubbling away on the stove, and he sprinkled a handful of the mint and cilantro on top.

Megan snapped her fingers. "Bibi, you're absolutely right. The flowers are a link. Claire had them. If they made it into poor Penny's makeshift grave, and if Olive is to be believed and they never found Claire, then whomever killed Penny knows where Claire is."

"Unless Claire is the killer."

Megan stared at her grandmother. It would explain both Claire's disappearance and the flowers.

Bibi washed her hands and dried them with a fresh towel. "I think I'm through here, Megan. And you know what I haven't done yet?"

"What's that?" Megan asked cautiously.

"I haven't paid my respects to the von Tressler family. As an old woman in this town, I should probably do that, don't you think?"

Megan grinned. Leave it to Bibi. "I think that's a swell idea. In fact, propriety demands it."

*   *   *

While Bibi got changed, Megan headed up to the Marshall place to speak with Ryan. Despite the fact that it was nearly three o'clock on a Saturday, she knew she'd find her contractor and his crew working. They were under a deadline, and she had paid a premium to get the work done this summer. She was surprised to find Ryan alone in the house's center hall. He was taking window measurements, a small notebook, and a pencil on a ladder nearby. He looked up in surprise when Megan entered the room, squinting those piercing blue eyes.

"What brings you here? I figured you'd be doing farm-y things on a gorgeous day like today."

Megan smiled. "I went to the farmers market this morning, but since then, I've been a little distracted, as you can imagine."

"Farm work waits for no one."

"Indeed." Megan walked around the entry hall, inspecting the work. Ryan and his team had replastered the walls, sanded and refinished the original quarter-sawn oak floors, and now he was putting new period-appropriate trim around the replacement windows. The center hall led into a living room on one side and a small dining room on the other. Behind the living room was a tiny kitchen that the contractors had blown out to make it larger and more modern. The caretaker's apartment was being constructed off the kitchen—two bedrooms and a large kitchen/dining area/living area. It was all coming together—slowly. "I like what you've done."

Ryan wiped his hands on dusty cargo pants. "It does look better, doesn't it?" He glanced around the room, his gaze trailing into the living room. "This will be nice when it's finished." He eyed Megan with a sideways glance. "But I'm guessing you're not here about the work."

"No, I'm not."

"Brian Porter told you what we found?"

Megan nodded. "Can you show me where you found it?"

"One of my men actually found it, but I can show you the general vicinity."

Ryan arranged the notebook and pencil neatly next to one another on the ladder before wiping his hands again with the towel. "Follow me."

Megan trailed her contractor out the front door and around to the side of the house where the Bilco doors were. Ryan pointed at the area near the doors. "There."

Megan examined the spot. The area was a main thoroughfare for the construction crew, and the little grass there was had been trampled on. Bald patches of clay-like mud dotted the area, and in those patches, Megan could make out scores of tread marks. So much for getting shoe prints.

"Just sitting there?"

"Yep. A little crumpled and dirty. Lou, that's one of my guys, was about to toss it when I noticed what he was doing. Figured since that body showed up, we should tell you about it. Then when I opened it...well, I'm sorry. It's not right to find something sentimental discarded that way."

Megan scanned the yard for any other items, but Ryan was a meticulous contractor and she only saw a few tools stacked neatly against the side of the house.

"Nothing else near that paper, huh? No other items, no discernable footprints, nothing."

"Nothing. Just the paper."

Megan felt her shoulders tighten. She had no reason to doubt Ryan, but she felt at her core like she was overlooking something.

"The police been by yet?" she asked. "If not, expect one of

King's officers to come by to check up on the obituary."

"No police since yesterday. Only person I saw here was that woman."

"*That woman?*"

"The woman who came by on Wednesday. The one with the red hair."

Olive Dunkel? "When was she here?"

"This morning. I told her you were at the farmers market. She find you?"

"She found me alright." Megan said, "You said she came by on Wednesday?"

"Yeah, she was with the other woman, the one who...the one who died. They were looking for you then, too."

That was the night Penny and her sister Olive showed up at the restaurant to ask about Claire. "Bibi said they called."

"I don't know anything about a call. They pulled up, asked where you were, and left. They seemed agitated, especially the blonde. I told them I had no idea where you were."

"Is it possible the redhead left this here this morning when she came by?"

Ryan stared off in the distance, hands on his hips, considering Megan's question. "I don't think so. I was outside with Lou and Maurice when she drove up. She got out of her car and yelled at us from across the yard. Then she left. She wasn't walking around or anything."

But she knew where Megan's house was. And she knew where the Marshall property was. And she probably knew where her sister's body had been placed. How many times had she come by when no one was there? Or when Bibi was home alone?

"What do you want me to say if she comes back again?" Ryan asked.

"Nothing," Megan said. "Tell her nothing. Just call me right away."

Nine

"Remember, Megan, we're here to pay our respects. I couldn't come on Wednesday because I was under the weather so you agreed to bring me by today." Bibi elbowed Megan. "Got it?" She winked.

"Got it."

"Let me do the talking."

"You've said that several times, Bibi. I understand."

Bibi had changed into a black dress and a pair of black low heels. She'd even put on her best faux pearls for the occasion. On her lap was a basket of baked goods she'd thawed from the freezer—cookies and pumpkin bread and a loaf of her coveted sourdough. Megan would have been impressed except for the cane her grandmother had also brought along, a cane she only seemed to use when she wanted people to underestimate her.

"You're really getting into this role playing," Megan said. "I'm surprised you didn't bring your walker and stash a gun in your handbag."

"I thought about it." She glanced across the truck's cabin at Megan, a disapproving frown on her face. "You could have done a more convincing job."

She was referring to Megan's choice of clothes—plain black pants and a dusty pink sleeveless blouse. Bibi had wanted her to change into mourning clothes before leaving the house but finally agreed to go when Megan promised they'd stop for ice cream on the way home.

Megan pulled in front of the von Tressler house. She got a clearer view in the sunnier weather. The house's beige façade was fronted by a white porch that ran the width of the house. White columns stretched to a second story piazza, and beyond that, a flat roofline. A gardener standing by a potting shed was taking advantage of the weather and planting a line of shrubs around the perimeter of the house. The circular driveway was clear of vehicles today. Nevertheless, it felt like déjà vu.

"Wow," Bibi said, "who thought building this place was a good idea?"

"The von Tresslers."

"These are the people who stole our contractor."

"In a manner of speaking." Megan glanced at her grandmother. "Please don't bring that up."

"Little old helpless me?" Bibi waved her hand in front of her face. "I would never do anything contrary."

"*Yeah, right.*"

"Just let me do the talking."

The uniformed woman who answered the door regarded Megan and her grandmother with polite disdain.

"I'm afraid Mrs. von Tressler is not accepting company today."

"Oh, that's too bad. I brought her this and was hoping to give it to her in person." Bibi glanced at Megan. On cue, Megan held up the basket. Bibi leaned on her cane and touched the basket with a free hand. "I made everything myself."

The woman's expression softened. "Well, that was kind of you. I can give it to Mrs. von Tressler on your behalf. As I'm sure you can understand, she's still in mourning—"

"Let them in, Margot," said a voice from inside.

It was a surprisingly deep voice, almost sultry, and Megan strained to see beyond the maid.

The woman named Margot gave a curt nod and held the door open. Megan helped Bibi navigate the step up into the foyer. They entered into a white tiled, two-story hall. A circular staircase wound off to the right. In the center of the room sat a single round table, and on it, an arrangement of white and yellow flowers. No art adorned the walls.

A small Cavalier King Charles Spaniel trotted out to meet them. She sniffed Megan, then Bibi, before plopping herself down at Bibi's feet.

"She already knows who the easy one is," Megan whispered.

Bibi elbowed her gently in the side.

"Lulu, come here."

The dog ran to the far end of the hall. Standing in the entryway to what appeared to be a library or office was a woman in her early sixties wearing a tailored gray sheath dress and matching cardigan. Layered, short white hair framed a strong, boxy jawline and sharp nose. Probing green eyes hinted at an iron will even as the woman smiled a welcome, a smile meant for Bibi although her gaze was on Megan. The woman crossed the room in three strides and held out her hand to Bibi.

"I'm Veronica Maplewood, Melanie's mother. Are you friends of my daughter?"

"Bonnie Birch. We're from town," Bibi said. "We own Washington Acres, the farm and café."

"Nice that you came to see Melanie." Her speech was ever so slightly slurred. Megan caught the unmistakable scent of bourbon on her breath.

Bibi hunched over her cane. "I'm afraid I couldn't make the

memorial because of my sciatica and my gout, so we thought we would come by today. My granddaughter, Megan, drove me over. I can't drive because of my sciatica and my gout, you see."

Megan fought hard not to roll her eyes. She shook hands with Veronica, noting the dry, limp grasp, and shot her grandmother an exasperated sideways glare.

"Is Melanie here?" Bibi asked. "We brought her a basket of goodies, and I would just love to give her this in person. She's such a dear." Bibi flashed a warming smile and added, "We just adore her."

Veronica's eyebrows knit together. She looked at Bibi as though she were trying to figure out whether she was being sincere. "My daughter has a migraine, I'm afraid. Margot will put the basket in the kitchen. Melanie will enjoy these later, when she's up."

"Oh, I'm sure things have been difficult for her," Bibi said. "What with David and then everything."

"*Everything*?" Veronica asked. She made a small hiccup and covered her mouth with her hand. "What do you mean by everything?"

"The move, construction. We all know how very stressful that can be. And then with that woman just disappearing out of thin air? Troubling for anyone, much less a woman who just lost her beloved." Bibi shuffled her feet and leaned harder on her cane. "Do you mind if I sit? My legs aren't what they used to be."

"Of course."

Megan followed Veronica and her grandmother into a white and ecru-decorated living room. Bibi hobbled along as though she would topple over at any moment. Megan hoped Veronica never stopped by the café to witness the same Bonnie Birch standing in a hot kitchen for hours on end, cover blown.

"Sit, please." Veronica motioned toward the couch

"Thank you, my dear. You young people don't know what it's like." She shook her head. "Getting old is so tiresome."

"I'm not that young," Veronica said, but the slightest smile had broken through the brittle veneer.

"Oh, you're young." Bibi rubbed at her right leg for effect. "Very young."

"Would either of you like something to drink?" asked the maid. "Iced tea, perhaps?"

"I'd love an iced tea," Bibi said to Veronica. "Thank you."

"I'll have my usual," Veronica said. "On the rocks. And an iced tea for Mrs. Birch."

Bibi nodded approvingly. After a moment, she said, "Your daughter—does she get migraines frequently?"

"Not really, but the stress of the last week has gotten to her. That's why I'm here."

"We feel so bad for your daughter. To lose the love of your life at such a tender age. It must be so hard."

"She's doing what she can. Focusing on the dog, the house. Her future."

Bibi made a show of looking around. "This house. It's so lovely." Bibi smiled. "Just grand."

Veronica frowned. "It's a lot of house. Too much, if you ask me. But no one did."

"Melanie must have had fun designing it," Bibi said.

"It was mostly David, her husband." Veronica glanced around the living room. "And the décor was done by his designer. Very austere and a bit ostentatious, if you ask me. But again, no one did." She kneaded her hands together, glanced toward the entry hall as though looking for the maid.

"Is this your first time in Winsome?" Bibi asked.

"Oh, no. I came when they first chose this town. Why, I asked them. It's quaint, but you'll both get bored. They were used to the city life, to a penthouse apartment downtown." She smiled, and Megan saw the first hint of maternal pride. "They were living well in Philadelphia."

"Are you from Pennsylvania?" Megan asked.

"Oh, lord, no. I was born in Chicago and raised in California."

"And now?" Bibi asked. "Where is home?"

Veronica crossed her legs. "New Jersey, outside of New York City. I prefer cities. The culture, the arts. So does my daughter."

"Then why Winsome?" Bibi asked.

"Why, indeed? Because this is what *David* wanted."

"It must be refreshing to enjoy the country life for a bit," Bibi said. She looked at Megan, eyebrows arched. "Getting away from it all and such."

"I'm not sure I'd use the word 'refreshing.'" Veronica pursed thin lips. "Anyway, I came for a few days to help with David's memorial, and I hope to leave this week."

Margot returned with a tray of iced teas, ginger cookies, napkins, silver spoons, one caramel-colored drink, and Sugar in the Raw. Bibi accepted an iced tea. Megan could see her grandmother eyeing up the cookies. Her sweet tooth knew no bounds.

"So how do you two know Melanie?" Veronica asked. She took a long sip of her drink, her shoulders relaxing as she drank. "I know you said you're from Winsome, Bonnie, but did you know David?"

"David was a regular customer at our café. I'd see him there often."

Megan watched her grandmother fib without batting an eye.

"Oh, really?" Veronica said. "David seemed like a bit of a

hermit to me. Maybe your café is really good."

"I don't like to brag," Bibi said. She took a dainty swallow of tea. "But it is."

"So you only knew him as a customer?"

"That, and he and your daughter stole our contractor." Bibi's voice was maple syrup sweet. Megan's neck snapped in her grandmother's direction.

After recovering from her obvious surprise, Veronica said, "Would that be the contractor who disappeared with funds that didn't belong to him? I'd say my daughter and David did you a favor."

"No one knew that at the time." Bibi took another sip of iced tea. "But that was then. Now Melanie is a neighbor and Winsome community member and we're here to support her."

"That's very kind of you."

Somewhere in the house, a phone rang.

"Okay, then." Veronica started to rise—clearly, Megan thought, she's had enough of this charade—when Bibi beat her to it.

"Do you have a bathroom nearby?" Bibi asked. "I'm afraid this tea has gone right through me."

Veronica glanced at Bibi's glass, which was still full. "Of course," she said stiffly. "Margot can show you where it is. Margot!"

The maid appeared out of nowhere, and while she led Bibi back out into the hall, Megan busied her hands by taking a glass of tea. "It's a lovely house," Megan said. "Very peaceful."

"Oh, please. It's an awful house," Veronica said. "David wanted Greek Revival, Melanie wanted French Colonial, and the offspring of their unforgivable compromise is this architectural bastard." She shook her head. "Look, I appreciate that you and your grandmother came to pay your respects to Melanie, but I'm well aware that the town of Winsome holds no love for the von Tressler family."

"That's not true," Megan said. The words sounded flaccid, even to her.

"David wasn't a people person. He moved here to get away from family drama and because, frankly, property is cheaper. My daughter went along for the ride."

"Winsome is a nice place to live and raise a family."

"It's also a nice place to feel superior. When you have too much of Daddy's money and zero humility, you can convince yourself that you're better than those with fewer dollars in the bank. The von Tressler men were very good at placing themselves in little ponds. They liked being the big fish, and although they were rich, it didn't take much in places like New York City or even Philadelphia to remind them that others were richer."

Her words came out with such vehemence that Megan moved physically backwards against the couch. Clearly there was little love lost between Veronica Maplewood and her daughter's family, and with alcohol in her hand and her belly, Veronica seemed only too happy to voice her opinions. Megan thought back to the scene at Merry's where this all began. Was it possible that the woman who would "eat Claire alive" was Veronica, not Melanie?

"Mrs. Maplewood—"

"Ms. Maplewood. I haven't been a missus in over fifteen years."

"Ms. Maplewood, did you know Claire, David's stepmother?"

Veronica's face seemed to shrink in on itself in anger. Her mouth twisted into a sneer. "Of course."

"I dropped her off at this house the day of the memorial,

but her sister Olive says she never arrived."

Veronica stood. She walked stiffly toward the built-in bookshelves at the back of the room. A set of silver-framed wedding photos sat next to a stack of pristine coffee table books. "Claire wasn't here. I would have known had she been here." Veronica turned quickly. "Where is your grandmother?" she asked, shifting the topic. "Do you think she's okay?"

"She's fine. Things take her longer these days."

"Perhaps we should check on her. Margot!"

While Veronica left the room to ask Margot to check on Bibi, Megan studied the photographs. The first was of Melanie and David in a white-ensconced horse drawn carriage. The young bride wore a pale pink sleeveless dress, very chic and very expensive-looking. The groom, many years her senior, wore a black tuxedo and sported a closely-cropped beard. The second photo was of the bride and groom with what Megan could only assume were their parents: Veronica and another couple next to Melanie and Claire and a hunched over gentleman in his seventies or eighties next to David. Only David was smiling.

"That's Melanie's father—my ex-husband—and his fourth wife. Karma got the best of him. At sixty-six, he and his Viagra fathered another baby." Veronica had returned. She laughed bitterly from behind Megan. "While I fly to Maui, he's mopping up vomit."

Megan didn't know what to say, so she said nothing.

"Your grandmother got confused. Margot found her in the kitchen. They're coming now."

Megan thanked her. "We'll get going. Please give Melanie our condolences."

Veronica stood by Megan, looking at the family wedding photos from behind Megan's back. Megan could hear the shuffle-clomp of Bibi and her cane heading their way across the tile floor.

"You look lovely in that picture," Megan said. She meant it. Veronica seemed young and vivacious, especially next to David and his father.

"We were happy then. The union between Melanie and David held such promise. A new beginning for my daughter, a new opportunity to make something of herself." She shook her head. "Karma again, I guess."

Megan glanced at Veronica. "Karma?"

Veronica looked reluctant to elaborate. She twirled her glass, watching as the ice cubes floated in the brown liquid. She brought the glass to her lips and drained it in one long swallow.

"Karma?" Megan repeated.

Veronica waved her glass at Margot, asking for another. "David doesn't have a history of being faithful. Melanie was neither his first nor his last affair."

"Ah."

Bibi leaned against the wall and called Megan's name. "Time to go."

Megan held up a hand. "I'm sorry to hear that," she said to Veronica, "but David's death...well, I don't think karma is *that* heavy handed."

Veronica's eyes widened in surprise. "His death?" Her laugh was shrill and mean. "No, not that...his death was due to too many hamburgers and late-night gin and tonics. I'm talking about Claire," she whispered.

"Claire?"

"It takes two to tango. And tango with a married man she did."

Megan and Bibi were silent for the first five minutes of the trip back to Washington Acres. Megan ran through her conversation with Veronica in her head, organizing her thoughts. She assumed the married man Claire had been tangoing with was David. Why would Veronica share something so intimate about her son-in-law and Claire? It was clear Veronica didn't like David, nor did she seem to approve of the big house or the move to Pennsylvania. Was it just the booze talking...or was there more to her behavior?

Bibi seemed to be jotting notes in a notebook she kept in her bottomless bag.

"I'll start," Bibi said when she'd finished writing. "It's obvious Ms. Veronica Maplewood does not like the von Tressler home."

"I don't think she was too crazy about David, either. She basically called him egotistical and snobbish. And an adulterer." Megan shared what Veronica had said right before they left. "So David and Claire _were_ having an affair. I thought so, but Veronica basically confirmed it."

"Did she talk about Claire?" Bibi asked.

"Only to deny seeing her at the memorial."

"What did you think of Veronica?" Bibi asked. "Reliable?"

"I guess—other than the booze. After you left the room, she opened up a bit more. She seems bitter and not particularly nurturing toward her daughter." Megan turned onto the road that led to Washington Acres. "She painted Melanie as another woman who makes questionable choices. Her attitude toward her daughter's choices seemed cold and pragmatic." Megan flashed back to the wedding photos. "It seems that David and Melanie got together while David was still married."

"Adultery runs in the family?"

"Perhaps." Megan slowed to honor a stop sign. The evening air had grown heavy with dark clouds sullying the sky. An evening thunderstorm seemed likely. More rain, more mud. "Other than that—and a glimpse of the inside of the mansion—it was kind of a wasted trip."

"I'm not so sure about that. When I went to the bathroom, which was a ruse by the way, I didn't have to go, I looked out back through the kitchen window. And what a kitchen, Megan. Two islands. *Two.* Who needs two islands?"

"The window, Bibi. What did you see?"

"Melanie. She was sunbathing in the backyard."

"Maybe that's how she rids herself of a migraine."

"I guess." Bibi made a *tsk*, *tsk* sound. "Did taking her top off help her, too?"

"I guess we won't know since she wouldn't talk to us. We can't really go and give our condolences again."

Megan pulled into the driveway and cut the engine.

"I took care of that." Bibi smiled slyly.

Megan's heart beat a little faster. "What did you do?"

"I'm so forgetful, Megan. I left my good pearls in their bathroom."

Megan patted her grandmother's leg. "You're a genius. Now we have an excuse to go back."

Bibi nodded. "But not right now. Right now you need to start the truck and turn around."

Megan rolled her eyes, a gesture she'd been holding in for hours. "For what?"

"Ice cream. You promised."

Ten

Megan didn't have to go to Melanie von Tressler; Melanie came to her.

Late Sunday mornings at the café were the busiest time of the week. Locals and visitors alike came after church, doctors and nurses and night-shift workers from the local factories came after work, and the few partygoers who had stayed up all night joined for a hangover special. Megan had all hands on deck to handle the crowd—Bibi and Alvaro in the kitchen, Emily at the register, and Megan and Clover handling orders. The café didn't really offer a brunch menu; it was more of a lunch or breakfast menu, and in the heat of this early July morning, Alvaro's chilaquiles paired with a soothing breakfast smoothie were all the rage.

So when someone at the copper-topped counter ordered a single piece of rye toast and a cup of coffee from behind a newspaper, Megan took notice.

A slim, pale hand slid Bibi's necklace across the counter before dropping the newspaper.

"Melanie. Thank you."

Melanie regarded Megan coolly, and Megan returned the stare. Melanie was a slim woman of average height. White-blond bangs framed a round face. Her round, full mouth was pressed into a pout, green eyes narrowed in anger. Up close and in person, she looked even younger than her forty-ish years—younger and less friendly. "My mother said you were looking for me?"

"We came to give our condolences."

"Is that right?" Melanie tilted her head. "I saw your grandmother staring at me through the kitchen window."

"Your mother told us you had a migraine."

"My mother exaggerates." Melanie tapped at the countertop with a French-tipped nail. "Thank you for the basket, but I wasn't born yesterday. Everyone in this town resents us being here. The only person who came to David's memorial was that woman from the flower shop, and I *know* she was just being nosy." Melanie sniffled. "You too? Were you and your grandmother trying to get a glimpse of the house? Wanted to see the weirdos who had moved to the top of the hill?"

"That's not it at all," Megan said truthfully.

"I know about Penny, Claire's sister. The police practically barged in to talk to me. I know she was found on your farm. That was awful, but if you came about that, I had nothing to do with it."

Clover walked behind Megan and tapped her on the shoulder. Megan nodded. A line had formed outside the café, and Clover couldn't handle the influx of customers on her own.

"Look, Melanie, let me get you some food. I can't talk now, but—"

"There's nothing else to say. You came, you had your reasons, your grandmother left her necklace, and I'm returning it." She ran a hand through her bangs. "I'll still take that toast and coffee."

"How about the chilaquiles? They're a little more substantial." Megan smiled. "On the house."

"Just toast. But on the house would still be nice." Melanie

picked up the newspaper. "And maybe we can go for a walk after your shift is over. I've changed my mind. A talk might be good after all."

Megan walked away wondering what had just happened.

By one thirty that afternoon, the lunch crowd had gone and only one table was still occupied. Clover and Megan had the dining area cleaned up for dinner, and Bibi and Alvaro were rearranging the kitchen for the evening regulars. Sunday nights weren't generally crowded, but the café had its regular Sunday set, mostly singles and couples who didn't feel like cooking. Alvaro normally made comfort food on Sundays, and tonight's roast chicken was perfuming the air and making Megan's stomach grumble.

"I heard that," Clover said. "Eat something, please. In fact, why don't you pack up and head home. It's late, and I know you have stuff to do at the farm." She stole a surreptitious look back at the kitchen. "Or maybe you could spend some time with Denver. Haven't seen as much of him lately."

"As a matter of fact, Denver and I have plans for tonight. He's taking me to the city for a concert and dinner."

"Ooh, that sounds like fun. That little farm to table place on the Parkway?"

"Nope." Megan finished wiping down the last of the counter. "I've been craving seafood, so we're going to a little hole in the wall. Fish and chips, that sort of thing."

"Sounds good." Clover's attention wandered to the front of the store. "Speak of the devil, look who just walked in."

Megan looked up in time to see Denver heading their way with Roger Becker, the town's zoning commissioner. Denver grinned when he saw Megan. Roger waved.

"Go," Clover said. "We're good here."

Megan grabbed her purse from under the counter, bid Bibi and Alvaro good-bye, and met Denver by the store's cash register, where he was a captive audience to Roger's chattiness. Megan caught the tail-end of what he was saying.

"I just don't understand it. It's barely been any time at all." Roger, a tall, lanky man with a ring of dark hair, knew everyone and everything that was going on. He liked to tell people that he was in the business of knowing the whole town's business. "I guess you heard, Megan."

"Heard what?"

"The von Tressler home is going up for sale."

"But they just built that thing."

Roger nodded solemnly. "I was just telling Denver here that Melanie isn't staying in Winsome. Her mother wants her to move back to New Jersey with her." His eyes grew round behind his glasses. "Have you met that mother, Megan? Whew. Wouldn't want to meet *her* under an overpass."

Not quite the saying, Megan thought, but having met Veronica Maplewood, she knew what he meant. "Does Melanie want to leave?"

"Does it matter?" Roger whistled. "I heard they spent over three million building that house—more if you count the money their contractor absconded off with. It's a fine house, but people who can afford a three-million-dollar house either want a piece of restored history or they want to design their own oversized money pit. She'll never get their money back out, not if they sell now."

"It sits on a pretty piece of property high up on that hill," Denver said. "Who knows what city person will come along and want a view like that."

"Maybe, but I bet it stays for sale for a long time. Unless

she's willing to sell it at a significant loss."

"I hate the thought of it being abandoned," Denver said. "That's not good for the owner, and it's not good for the town."

"Right," Roger said. "Look what happened to von Tressler Senior's house." Another head shake.

"You mean Martin von Tressler's house? What happened?" Megan asked.

Roger leaned against the checkout counter as though settling in for a long story. He folded his arms over his chest. "The old man died, and no one wanted to live there. It just sits there decaying. A gorgeous property, from what I hear. Not sure why the old man's wife doesn't move back in." Roger leaned in and lowered his voice. "Did you know she's missing? I heard she never made it to the memorial. Just ran off."

"I've heard similar," Megan said, not wanting to get into the details.

"And then her sister was murdered. What is the world coming to?" Roger shook his head slowly back and forth.

"Maybe it makes sense that Melanie wants to sell," Denver said. "She lost her husband, her mother-in-law is missing, and then the murder."

"Maybe she's afraid she's next," someone behind them said.

They all turned to look at the source of the voice. Melanie was standing in between a shelf of organic canned goods and display of flours and baking ingredients. In jeans, a tank top, and sneakers, with her hair in a ponytail, she looked more like a teenager than a recent widow.

"She's right," Denver said, turning to acknowledge her. "Hello, Melanie. I can understand that you would be worried given all you've been through with your family."

"Family is kind of a stretch," Melanie said. "Penny hated me. She hated David, too." Quickly, she added, "That doesn't mean I wanted her dead."

"Of course not," Roger said. "We're sorry about your husband. We're sorry for what your family is going through."

Melanie's face remained blank. "Megan," she said. "That walk?"

Megan glanced at Denver. To Melanie, she said, "I'm afraid I need to take a pass—"

"Actually, Megs, I swung by to tell you I have a sick mare I need to see to. How about if I call you when I'm done and we'll head downtown. We have some time before we need to get on the road."

Megan nodded slowly, unsure if he actually had a sick mare or if he was buying her the ability to talk to Melanie.

Melanie clapped her hands. "Great. Let's go then."

Roger, clearly unwilling to end his audience with Winsome's most ostentatiously wealthy resident, said, "How is the house sale coming along?"

"I'm not selling."

"I heard that your mother—"

"My mother doesn't make decisions for me," Melanie said. "David and I built the house, and I intend to stay here. I just have some things I need to work out."

Roger looked like he'd just been slapped. He put a hand on his reddened cheek and said, "Great. We're happy to hear that."

"Are you?" Melanie looked from Roger to Denver to Megan. "Can we go?" she said to Megan.

Megan hesitated, but only for a second. Her curiosity about Melanie von Tressler and her odd family—and their potential connection to her—outweighed her annoyance at Melanie's petulant tone.

The air outside felt hot and oppressive compared to the coolness of the café. Megan regretted her decision not to change before leaving—her work clothes felt sticky and cloying. She walked alongside Melanie for a few minutes, watching the other people walking along the canal as her brain spun with questions.

She was thinking about Penny Greenleaf when Melanie said, "Your farm manager, Clay. Could I borrow him for a while?"

Megan could not hide her astonishment. "*Borrow* him?"

"We have so much work that still needs to be done around the house. That's one of my mother's issues. She thinks I won't be able to handle it. I thought with someone who knows Winsome at the house, I could take care of the remaining to-dos." She glanced at Megan. "You and I are about the same age. It can be hard to get contractors to take you seriously. A guy would help."

Megan was too stunned to speak. Melanie seemed completely tone deaf to what she was asking for. And this after she and her late husband pulled Megan's contractor away from the Marshall house project—some nerve, Megan thought.

Megan was trying to choose words that didn't have only four letters, when Melanie said. "Or the other one. The other guy at your farm? I could borrow him. Is he handy?"

Megan stopped walking. Hands on her hips, she said, "His name is Brian. You do realize that it's the middle of growing season, and I need my farm manager and my farm hand."

"It would just be for a few weeks. Even a few days would help."

"Even if I said okay—which I am absolutely not doing—they're capable of making their own decisions. And anyway, you don't need a man around to find contractors, Melanie. You're capable of doing that yourself."

"I've offended you."

Megan took a deep breath. "Yes, you've offended me."

Melanie hit her head lightly with the palm of her hand. "My mother always tells me I'm terrible with people. That's why she didn't want me to greet you and your grandmother. Thanks for the basket, by the way." She grimaced. "I tried to be friendly toward Claire, and look how that turned out. You and I are near the same age—right? This should be way easier than it is."

"It shouldn't be easy to ask another person for their loyal employees, Melanie. That's not how the world works. Like Duke, your contractor. I had already signed him for a project. I'd given him a deposit. You and David came along and outbid everyone in Winsome. I—many of us—had to pay a premium to go outside our area for help." Megan fought to keep her voice under control. She hadn't realized how much their actions had infuriated her. "You swooped in, didn't speak to anyone in town, not really, and pulled that stunt. You wonder why you got the cold shoulder from the good people of Winsome. Maybe that was why."

Melanie regarded Megan, unblinking. It's never occurred to her that her actions had consequences for other people, Megan thought. She really is that self-absorbed.

"I don't know what to say." Melanie glanced around, not meeting Megan's gaze. A child on a tricycle zoomed past them. Melanie watched her pedal down the pathway, a frown marring pretty features. "Forget I asked. Can you do that? Can we start over?"

Megan sighed. Could she do that? She wanted answers, so she supposed she needed to. At least a little.

"Do you have a job?" Megan asked. "Something that keeps you occupied during the day?"

"Not really. I used to be in sales. That's how I met David. We worked together and went to the same country club." She perked up. "Do you have a country club in Winsome?"

"No. You'd have to go to a nearby town for that."

"Oh." Her face fell. "David had things planned for us. Travel. The house. He was semi-retired, so we could spend time doing other things."

"Semi-retired? I thought he worked for his father's business?"

"Oh, he did. You may have heard of it? Von Tressler Investments."

"I have." Megan started walking again, away from the café. She wanted to keep Melanie talking. "What did he do there?"

"Everything at one point or another. Chief Operating Officer overseeing the furniture business—that's how they got started, selling furniture. Before his father died, he became CEO for a bit."

"Before he semi-retired?"

Melanie was quiet for a moment. They were passing a shady spot by the canal, where a large maple tree intersected the path. A bench had been placed underneath the tree by the town's Beautification Board—a bench that was currently empty. "Want to sit?" Melanie asked.

"Sure."

Melanie sank down on the bench with a huff. "The official reason he retired is that he wanted to spend more time with me. Younger wife, older man, maximizing time together. David had some health issues—bad ticker, high cholesterol, nothing major. He said he was ready to take things slow, enjoy life. You get it."

Megan got it. "And the real reason?"

Another sigh, this one louder. "He'd had an affair with his own stepmother." Melanie closed her eyes. "Everyone at the headquarters knew it. So much gossip. It soured his relationship with Martin, made both of them miserable. He couldn't stay. His nephew took over as CEO."

"His nephew?"

"His late sister's son, Dominick von Tressler. Martin and his daughter never got along, but Dominick is a lot like Martin. It all worked out eventually."

Melanie recited this as though she hadn't been involved at the time. "And you?" Megan asked gently. "Did it work out for you?"

Melanie's laugh sounded forced. "Claire really loved him. I mean, she *really* loved David. Too bad he didn't love her in the same way." Melanie stretched long, lean legs out in front of her. "If you ask me, she'd fallen in love with David before she married Martin. The von Tressler men must have seemed larger than life to an uneducated girl like Claire. But Claire is feisty. And vindictive. I'll give her that—she has spirit."

"How did they meet?"

"Through Martin. Claire had been Martin's assistant. Cliché, maybe, but sometimes things happen. He married the help. I don't know that Claire ever really loved Martin. When he got bored with her—how could he not?—she got angry. What better way to get back at your husband than by bedding his son?"

"You don't seem terribly upset."

"I was at the time. My husband and his stepmother? I mean seriously, how much more humiliating can it get? I threatened to leave David, but we had a prenup, and you know how that goes. I leave, I get nothing." She shrugged. "Anyway, he apologized, we left Philadelphia, and we came here." Her expression soured. "To paradise."

"You don't love it here."

"We may only be an hour from the city, but if feels like we're in the middle of nowhere somedays."

Megan picked a maple leaf off the bench beside her. She ran

a finger across its surface, taking some solace in its simplicity. Listening to Melanie made her sad. She seemed like a woman trapped in her world of excess.

Megan said, "You have a lot of options. You could sell the house and do something you've always wanted to do. You could volunteer. You could invest in a new career. You're not helpless."

Melanie laughed. "I can't really sell that house. We spent way more on it than it would sell for. I know that. Especially because our contractor," she had the decency to flush, "especially because Duke never finished the recreation room in the basement, the landscaping, or the master suite." She threw her head back. "Three and a half million dollars and it's not done."

"So you take a loss."

"I told you I had a prenup. I can't afford a loss."

Megan chose her next words carefully. "David passed away. Surely you'll inherit his portion of the business."

Melanie stood up, stretched, and made a show of looking at her watch. "I need to get back before my mother has a stroke."

"It's nice that she worries about you."

Melanie didn't miss a beat. "Veronica Maplewood worries about no one but herself."

Eleven

"Fish and chips," Denver said, staring at the small menu in front of him. He and Megan were at Lou's, a mom and pop out of the way restaurant that specialized in two things: fish and fried foods. Their fish and chips was killer, as were their fish tacos.

"Fish tacos, please," Megan said. "Broiled." She watched as the waiter made his way across the small shack-like establishment, a place of scarred wood tables, mismatched chairs, and plastic-coated menus. There was always a crowd, but if you were willing to wait, you could get a table and a little Philadelphia ambiance to go with it.

"What time is the concert?" Megan asked.

"Doors open at eight." Denver took a long swig of beer. "First time at the Kimmel Center?"

Megan shook her head. She'd been there with Bibi before. Bibi loved orchestra music, and while she'd been reluctant to travel into the city lately, they'd gone a few times when Megan first moved to Winsome. Tonight was bittersweet. Megan had left Bibi dozing in front of the television, her knitting untouched by her side. She wished her grandmother would have agreed to join them, but more and more she seemed intent on giving them what she called "alone time."

"It's a nice night for a concert," Denver said. He reached across the small corner table and took Megan's hand. "No thunder and lightning, aye Megs?"

"What?"

"You're very distracted tonight. Everything okay?"

Megan smiled. "Things are fine. I think I'm just...it's just been a rough week."

"You're thinking of the woman who was found at your property."

"Am I that transparent?" Megan rubbed Denver's hand. Such large hands, she thought. Large and calloused and strong. "I'm thinking about Penny and why someone left her at the Marshall house. I'm thinking about Melanie von Tressler and how miserable she seemed today. I'm thinking about when I can get the Marshall house inn and barn up and running." She sighed. "And truth be told, I'm thinking about Claire, the woman I left at the memorial. No one has seen her, Denver. I know she was there. She had the flowers...the flowers that turned up in Penny's makeshift grave."

Denver didn't say anything. He turned Megan's hand over and traced the lines of her fingers and palm with his pointer finger. His touch was warm, comforting.

The waiter returned with some vinegar and ketchup and another beer for Denver. After he was gone, Denver said, "How is Bonnie faring?"

"Tough as nails—at least on the outside." Megan shared their visit to the von Tresslers. "She's like Nancy Drew's grandmother. If the situation didn't feel dire, I would be more amused."

"You're worried about her?"

"She's with Sadie, Gunther, and Sarge. That's a combined three-hundred-plus pounds of dog, two of whom are trained guard dogs. She'll be fine."

"That's not what I asked."

Megan looked into Denver's eyes. She saw her own worry reflected in his bright blues. "Yes. She's aging, I can see that. This is a lot for her, and sometimes I can tell she's in pain. At the same time, she resents my ministrations. She's an independent lady."

"I heard Porter is sleeping in the Marshall barn for a few nights. He asked me to take Sarge, but it sounds like Sarge would rather guard Bonnie down at the house."

It was true. When Megan left the house, Porter's German Shepherd had been sharing space with Sadie, next to Bibi. Megan wasn't sure if it was Bibi or Sadie the Shepherd preferred.

"Porter insisted. I didn't have the heart to say 'no.'"

Denver smiled, the dimples she loved so much in full view. "Maybe it's time to think about alternative arrangements."

Megan's stomach clenched, and her own smiled faded. She knew where this was headed. "Denver—"

"Hear me out." Denver removed his hand from hers and ran it through his thick hair, pushing it away from his face. "We've been together for a while now, and I think it's been a fine relationship."

Megan smiled. "*Fine*?"

Denver pressed on. "Maybe it's time to think about the next step."

Megan turned her head so she was looking at the table beside them. A man sat alone, staring at the menu. She shifted her gaze to the ground. She couldn't bear the need and want in Denver's eyes. She knew what he was getting at—marriage, kids. He'd hinted often enough. She loved him, but she couldn't take that next step. Not now. She'd been married once and look what happened. Soldier Mick, stolen from her in the prime of their life together. Mick, so full of youthful spirit and strength—until he wasn't. Megan believed herself to be a logical woman, and she knew this undercurrent of fear—terror, really—was just that, fear, but she felt helpless to control it.

"I have to think about Bibi."

"Your grandmother would always have a place with us, Megs. Or we could live with her at the farm. She would want this for you."

"You're a good man, Daniel."

"Ta," he said, sitting back in his seat. "I never trust what's going to come from your mouth when you use my God-given name."

"Nothing. You're a good man, and I love you. There is no one in this world I'd rather be with. Can't that be enough for now?"

"Two homes, sneaking around at night...the worry. If we were together, ye wouldn't need Porter living in your barn."

"I don't need Porter living in my barn now, and you know it." He'd hit a nerve, and Megan bit down to control the anger she was feeling, anger she knew was misplaced. "I don't *need* anyone."

"Oh, Megs, you're turning things around on me. That's not fair. Ye know what I mean." He lowered his voice. "I love ye, Megan Sawyer, as hard-headed as ye are. I accept you for who ye are, and I hope ye can see that. Moving in together, marriage, they won't change that."

Megan couldn't look him in the eye. The waiter arrived, and perhaps sensing the tension, quietly placed their meals in front of them and left without a word.

"Forget I said anything," Denver said after a pregnant pause. "You'll tell me when you're ready for something more." He reached for her hand, touched it lightly, and released it. "Okay? I'll trust that when the time is right, you'll let me know.

Let's just let it go."

Megan stabbed a piece of red cabbage with a fork, stealing a glance at her boyfriend. Denver's words were kind, but she knew him well enough to feel the steel in his tone, see the obstinate look in his eyes. She *wasn't* ready, and accepting that about herself had been a challenge. If he really did love her for who she was, he would need to accept it too. She shouldn't have to apologize for who she was.

So why did she feel so crappy?

"Forgotten," she said. "How's your fish?"

Denver, chowing down on haddock, didn't seem to hear her.

Twelve

The concert finished at eleven. It was a beautiful night, warm with just a touch of a breeze, lit by a blazing moon, and Megan didn't feel like going home just yet. The tension between them had gradually abated until they seemed back to normal. Still, Denver's words echoed in her head. She felt like she was failing him if she said no to taking the next step; she felt like she was failing herself if she said yes.

She told herself she would know when the time was right.

Outside the Kimmel Center, Megan turned on her phone, which had been off for the duration of the concert. No texts from Bibi, but she did have a text from Bobby King. *Call me*, was all it said. Sent at 9:19.

"Give me a minute," Megan told Denver. She dialed King's cell, but he didn't answer. "I wonder what he wanted."

"Maybe he has a lead on Penny's killer."

"Maybe."

Thinking about Penny made Megan think about Claire. When they were back in Denver's 4Runner, Megan said, "Would you mind a detour on the way home?"

"Sure. Where did ye want to go?"

She told him. His eyebrows lifted in surprise.

"Okay," he said, "but I want something in return."

"How about a sleepover?" Megan said.

Denver gave Megan a knowing half smile. "Tempting, but I thought I was getting a sleepover anyway."

"Breakfast in the morning? I'll personally make you French toast and fresh squeezed juice."

Denver smiled. Those dimples were back. "With real maple syrup—not that bottled imposter."

"With real maple syrup and some cinnamon on top."

"Maybe some whipped cream?"

She fake shoved him. "Now you're pushing it. But yes, real whipped cream. And butter. And any other artery-clogging substance you and my grandmother will insist on."

"Ta, I like you're cooking, so yes, we can take your detour. I just need an address."

That was more of a problem. "Give me a few minutes. I need to find it online."

Denver tapped his fingers on the dashboard. "I'm a patient man, Megs, but not that patient."

As Megan searched for Martin and Claire von Tressler's Philadelphia residence, she wondered whether she was projecting—or was there a double meaning behind Denver's words?

The von Tressler estate was in the Chestnut Hill area of Philadelphia. A three-story stone Colonial, it sat on a corner next to a historic Tudor with half as much acreage and twice the footprint. The house had a massive slate roof and a fieldstone wall that encircled a densely-landscaped property. Overgrown bushes reached out to the wide entry steps and kissed the front door. Perennial flower beds had returned to their wild roots and were rangy and overgrown. Someone was maintaining the lawn—but that was it. The streetlights and the glow from the moon provided enough light to the house to see by, but the dim light and moon shadows gave a spooky feel to the home's surroundings.

Denver parked along the street. Megan rolled down her window to get a better look. The neighborhood was dead quiet; most of the homes were dark except for outdoor lights and solar garden sconces. She didn't see a car in the von Tressler driveway, but then the driveway ran behind the house to a two-car detached garage shielded by shrubbery.

"The place looks haunted," Denver joked. "No lights on inside. No lights on outside."

Megan rolled up the window and opened the door to the 4Runner. Denver grabbed her arm gently. "Where are you going?"

"To look around."

"What if there's an alarm?"

"Then we'll hightail it out of here." She glanced around. "Besides, I don't see an alarm sign."

"I can't imagine there's no alarm."

"I don't think anyone lives here. Doesn't appear anyone has lived here for a while."

Denver frowned. "I'm coming with you."

Denver joined her on the sidewalk. Quickly, Megan walked to the side of the property, where the gate led behind the house. The gate was unlocked—in fact, it didn't seem to have a lock—and Megan opened it, holding it for Denver. Once inside the backyard, she started her phone's flashlight. The glow was weak, but between the moon and the flashlight, she could see several yards in every direction.

The backyard was as overgrown as the front. What must have once been a beautiful English-style garden with lush gardens, patches of grass, and welcoming stone benches, was now a mess of weeds and moss-covered furniture. The garage, a perfect miniature of the house, lay ahead, its doors closed and lights off. To their left was another fenced area. Inside was what looked like a pool—or a hole in the ground that used to be a pool. Megan shined her light on the hole. Ornate blue tiles stared up from under a few inches of slimy green water.

"What's that?" Denver hissed. He pointed to part of the property well beyond the garage and the pool, to an area surrounded by another fence, this one low to the ground and made of what looked to be wrought iron.

"Let's go see."

The sound of shuffling stopped her in her tracks.

"Rodents. Probably rats," Denver said. "Inside the garage. They won't hurt you."

They walked quietly to the edge of the garage. The yard seemed to stretch on forever, all of it reclaimed by nature. Megan hopped over an old wagon and followed a semi-hidden path between flower beds. No one was upkeeping the back of the property, presumably because it wasn't as visible to the neighbors and the gardens made it hard to manage. The grass was at least a foot high in places.

"Watch the glass over there," Denver whispered. "Broken window. Here." He took her hand. "Come this way."

Megan followed Denver through another small garden area. He skirted around a stone bench, then reached down and lifted Megan over it, too.

"Some of the stone is really slimy. I wouldn't touch it."

"Wasn't planning on it."

They reached the wrought iron fence and looked on in awe. It was a small graveyard. The stones were of varying sizes, but all encased by moss that came with age and the Philly humidity.

"It must be a family plot," Denver said.

"Is that even allowed?"

"I guess if it was here already."

"Now I know why this place feels so creepy." Megan shivered. She wrapped her arms around her chest and took a deep breath to calm her shaken nerves. "A graveyard, an overgrown garden, an empty pool."

"Not that this isn't fun, but what are you looking for?"

"I don't know."

"Very helpful."

Megan grabbed his hand. "This was Claire's house, the woman who disappeared. I guess I was hoping we'd find her here. Mystery solved and all that."

"If she's here, she's hiding. It looks like this place has been neglected for a while."

"I wonder why," Megan said, staring at the small graveyard. Who was buried here? Had this been the von Tressler family plot? "Who would purchase an estate with a cemetery on the premises?"

"A vampire?" When Megan didn't laugh, Denver said, "Not exactly welcoming." He scanned the rest of the immediate area with his own phone flashlight. "Want to check out the back of the house?"

Megan smiled. "I thought you were worried about an alarm system."

"No sirens yet."

"Let's walk the other way, on the far side of the pool."

Megan's light was stronger, so she picked her way through the overgrown gardens first, adhering to a narrow path along the rear of the stone wall. The smell of gardenia and lilies, normally scents she liked, overwhelmed her. Her exposed ankles stung from the grasses and nettles along the path. She was beginning to regret her idea.

They walked slowly, carefully, along the eastern wall. The pool area was visible beyond another row of untended hedges. On this side, a rose garden opened up to a square, rustic patio, its large stones swallowed by the grass and weeds that grew in between.

"Watch out for the thorns," Denver said. "They're catching my pants."

"Too late." Megan could feel warm blood on her exposed ankle.

Another shuffle and a shriek came from the darkness beyond the garage. Megan turned toward the sound and fell against a stone half-wall in the patio. She landed on both knees, hard.

"What the hell?" Her phone had fallen. She felt for it, found it in a nest of grass, and pointed it toward the stone object. "What was that?"

Denver knelt beside her. "Are you okay?"

"I'll be fine. What was that noise?"

"A bunny shrieking is my guess. Definitely animal, not human."

"You're sure?"

Denver hesitated. Only for a second, but she caught it. "I'm sure."

"What did I trip over?"

Denver helped her up. He shined his light on her legs. Torn capri pants, torn knees.

"Nothing urgent," Megan said. "I'm fine."

"We should get that cleaned up and disinfected."

"We will—later. What did I trip over?"

"Whatever it is, it smells."

Megan and Denver shined their lights into the structure. Stonework surrounded a small pool, its surface thick with rotting leaves and detritus. The whole thing was only about four feet by ten feet.

"It's a small lily pond. Probably pretty in its day," Denver said.

"Not pretty anymore."

Megan searched the ground for a stick. She found one lying in the rose bushes. Extracting it carefully, she used it to poke down into the pond. Bubbles rose to the surface—smelly bubbles.

"Methane." Denver took a step back.

"Surprisingly deep."

"Probably filled it with carp in the summer. Clearly no one's taking care of it now."

Megan dropped the stick back into the roses. "This whole place...what a waste."

A few minutes later, they made it to the back of the house. A sunroom lined half of its width, its windows shuttered to the outside world. A window to the left of the sunroom was closed and locked, but the shades weren't fully drawn.

"Shine a light in there," Denver said.

Megan obliged.

Denver used his height to peek into the window. "Can't really see anything. Seems empty."

Megan nodded. No signs of Claire. No signs of anyone.

Back in the 4Runner, Denver used his veterinarian supplies to clean and treat her wounded knees and ankle. "Flesh wounds," he said. "I'm more worried about your ankles. And we should check for ticks when we get back to the farm."

Megan agreed. Although her legs stung, she was glad they'd stopped by. The house had been beautiful once upon a time, she was sure, but although Martin von Tressler had only been dead a short time, it looked as though the house and gardens had been on the decline for a while. She had expected it to be empty. She hadn't expected it to look abandoned.

"These old houses are expensive to keep up," Denver said. "The roofs alone—all that slate." He made a whistling noise. "A small fortune. And the gardens and the pool? The house would take money most people will never see."

Megan didn't much care for fancy houses. Although grand, the place gave her the heebie-jeebies. She twisted around to give it a final glance. As she was turning back to face the road, something caught her eye. She drew a sharp breath. Was that a light in an upstairs window? Or a figment of her imagination? When she looked again, it was gone.

"Ye okay, Megs?" Denver asked. "Did ye see something?"

"No," Megan said. "Yes...I thought maybe...it was nothing."

"It's an evening for seeing things, for sure." Denver merged onto a main thoroughfare, then glanced over at her. "A haunted house like that? A person could go crazy living there alone."

Thirteen

July Fourth was to be a bittersweet holiday. That morning, Megan tucked the box of party favors she was going to use for the barn's grand opening into a cabinet in Bibi's sewing room. Maybe they could use them over Labor Day weekend, but she didn't think the red, white, and blue favors would work for the eventual opening. Her heart was heavy—she'd been looking forward to starting classes, and delaying the opening hit her wallet, too. The weather was clear so far, but Mother Nature could be cruel, and the weather predictors were promising thunderstorms just in time for all of those BBQs and picnics.

Megan could hear Bibi rustling around in her room. She closed the cabinet door and padded down the hall toward Bibi's quarters. It was after eight, and Bibi hadn't come downstairs yet—very unlike her. Megan knocked softly.

"You okay?"

"I'm fine, Megan."

"Can I come in?"

"Of course."

Megan opened the door slowly. Bibi was sitting in her recliner by the window, a brown and beige afghan over her legs and her knitting in her lap. When Megan entered, she smiled, eyes shining brightly.

"Good morning," Bibi said. "You look pretty this morning."

In lieu of the grand opening, Megan had agreed to set up a tent at the Winsome Canal Street sidewalk sale. She had changed from jeans and a grubby t-shirt to a lavender-colored vintage sundress for the event, and her shoulder-length brown hair, usually in a ponytail or pulled back from her face, was down and brushed today.

"I showered," she said.

Bibi laughed. "That's a start."

Megan settled on Bibi's bed. Her gaze was drawn to the cane, which was propped up against one of her bedside tables. "Are you feeling okay?"

"Just spending some quiet time in my room."

"You missed my French toast this morning. I even made whipped cream."

"It smelled good."

"Why didn't you come down? Because Denver was here?"

Bibi picked up her knitting. The *click, click, click* of her knitting needles, normally a pleasant sound, felt intrusive.

"Bibi?"

Bibi paused her knitting. "My legs ache, Megan. Somedays when the rain is coming, I can feel it in my bones. Today is one of those days." She glanced down at the afghan before adjusting it with arthritic fingers. "The steps can feel like a lot to navigate. I didn't want to go down and up again."

The old house had steep, narrow steps—typical for the period. Megan had been concerned for a while that at some point they would be too much for her grandmother. "Do you want me to put a lift in? Or maybe we could make the parlor into a bedroom."

"Oh gosh, no. I'm fine. I've just learned to be patient with my body."

"You're sure it wasn't because of Denver?"

Bibi tilted her head and gave Megan a look that married amusement and concern. "I adore Denver. You know that. And I always feel welcome with the two of you. He's become like a grandson to me. Stop fretting over me, Megan. When you hide things or fret it only makes me feel old."

"That wasn't my intent."

"I know. It's never anyone's intent." She sighed. "Look, I'll tell you when I need something, and you'll believe me when I do. That's all I ask." She smiled. "Okay?"

For the second time in two days, Megan felt emotionally off-kilter: first with Denver, now with Bibi. But Bibi was right, and she owed her the respect of taking her at her word. "Yes, of course. That's fair."

Bibi turned her attention back to the window. "It's nice out there now, but the weather will go awry soon. I feel it. What time are we expected at the Canal Street hoopla?"

"Sidewalk festivities start at ten."

"Then we should get ready."

Happily, Megan said, "You're still coming?"

"Did I tell you I wasn't?"

Megan stood and gave her grandmother a peck on the cheek. "You're getting cantankerous in your upper years."

"Not true," Bibi said. "I've been cantankerous for as long as I can remember."

Megan jogged up to the Marshall property before heading into town. Ryan was there, alone, working on the inside of the house. Entering, Megan felt like she was in a whole different space. The windows and trim were finished, the painting was complete, and Ryan was in the process of installing light fixtures—top hats and wall sconces. The overall effect was one of the past meets modern. Spacious and solid. Bright, but historically appropriate.

"Wow," Megan said. "Just wow."

"Like it?" Ryan couldn't hide his smile.

"Love it."

"Come here." He led Megan around to the back of the staircase. A small wooden desk had been built into the cubby underneath. "I even made you a check-in desk, with locking drawers for keys and files."

The desk was beautiful. Made of quarter sawn oak like the floors, it was simple in design but professionally crafted.

"And the top folds out, into the center hall, to create a small writing area for the guests while the innkeeper can sit comfortably in the cubby."

"I didn't ask for this, Ryan," Megan said. "I don't know what to say."

"I can take it out of you don't want it—"

"No, no, please don't. It's perfect. So thoughtful. It looks like it belongs with this old house."

"I felt bad...about everything you've been through."

"You're spending so much time here. I feel bad. You must have people at home who miss you."

Ryan picked up a broom and started sweeping invisible dirt on the floor. "I'm fine. Just a perfectionist."

Megan regarded her contractor. No ring, but she knew he had a significant other and at least one child. She wouldn't pry— it was none of her business. Still, she was curious.

"Why don't you take the rest of the day off?" Megan said.

"I know you want all of this done, and frankly, things aren't great at home. Being here takes my mind off of it."

"I'm sorry to hear that."

Ryan shrugged. "Life." He placed the broom against the wall. "You staying?"

His way of telling me to get lost, Megan thought. "No, I'm heading into town. Need anything?"

"Nah, but thanks for asking."

Megan thought of Duke, Melanie's contractor. Maybe Veronica had been right—she was lucky things had worked out the way they had.

As Megan was leaving, Ryan called after her. "That woman came back."

Megan spun around. "The red head?"

"Yes. I saw her standing outside the barn last night. Must have been around seven, eight o'clock."

"I thought you were going to call me."

Ryan looked chagrined. "I tried. Your phone rang straight through to voicemail. I called your house, and your grandmother answered. She didn't seem too concerned. Then your farm help arrived, and the woman left."

"What did she want? Did she say?"

"She was asking about the crime scene. Truth is, I felt kind of bad for her, losing her sister and all. She looked devastated."

"Yeah, she looked rough last time I saw her. She stopped here around eight you said?" When I was in the concert, Megan thought. I should never have gone. She'd turned her phone off. It went straight to voicemail, and somehow, she missed the missed call. I should have never left Bibi in the house alone, she thought—dogs or no dogs.

"Yeah, seven or eight." His eyes narrowed in concentration. "She did ask about you, come to think of it. How long you've lived here, whether you grew up in the area, other places you'd lived."

"What an odd thing to ask."

Ryan nodded. "I thought so, too. Didn't answer her, of course. I think that woman is a little off. Maybe you should tell

King. Let him check up on her."

"I'm sure he's already doing that." Megan's phone buzzed. It was a text from Clover asking when she would be at the café. "I have to go. If she returns, you know the routine."

Ryan saluted. "Enjoy your holiday."

"You, too."

Ryan had already turned back to his work, but Megan could hear him say, "Doubt it," as she left the house.

"You're late" Clover said. "I put out the beeswax candles, the locally-made soaps and lotions, those scarves your aunt wove, Bibi's hats—although they're out of season—and an assortment of organic and fair-trade chocolate. So far, so good. Want to put the jams and jellies out?"

"Sure, why not. And the pickled goods." Megan surveyed Canal Street. Downtown Winsome was a misnomer. There was only Canal Street, and on Canal there were only a dozen or so shops. But they were all leaning in today. Megan saw an impressive array of colorful tents, and even a salsa band outside the shoe store.

"Since when does Mrs. McCreeley play bongos?" Megan asked.

"Since Mr. McCreeley took up with their housekeeper."

"Ah."

Megan turned back to their table. It was sparse, but Clover had arranged things nicely. "Mind if I check on Alvaro and Bibi?"

"Go for it."

Inside, the atmosphere was festive. The café was crowded with people drinking coffee and iced drinks and eating the fresh doughnuts Alvaro had made for the occasion. The shop smelled of cinnamon and suntan lotion. Megan felt her mood lift.

"Fireworks tonight," Emily called from the register. "Clay and I are going. Want to join us?"

"I don't think so," Megan said.

"They're just along the canal. Should be fun."

Megan simply smiled. After the events of the last week, she wasn't sure her nerves could take the crowds or the explosions, but if Bibi wanted to go...she'd ask her.

Back in the kitchen, she found Bibi sitting on a chair, chopping scallions while Alvaro mixed his homemade masa harina with water to make tortillas.

"Mexican tonight?"

"Tacos. Fish, chicken, and cauliflower." Alvaro rolled the springy dough into a ball on a huge slab of marble. "Homemade tortillas, homemade salsa, homemade guacamole salad, and a side of beans and rice."

"Sounds delicious," Megan said.

Still kneading the tortilla dough, Alvaro nodded his head toward Bibi. "If Bibi will help me, churros for dessert."

"I'll help you, although none of this is very Fourth of July."

"Barbeque is overrated," Alvaro grumbled. "Besides, I have all that beautiful cauliflower Megan brought me. Cauliflower tacos, yes. Cauliflower burgers, no."

Megan couldn't argue. She gave her grandmother's arm a squeeze. "You want to stay for the fireworks tonight?"

"Maybe. By the time Alvaro is finished with all this non-traditional cooking, I may be exhausted."

Megan laughed. She was exhausted just listening to the menu.

"Megan," Emily said, popping her head into the kitchen, "Clover's looking for you."

"Be right there."

Bibi said, "Call Clay when you have time. He rang the café phone about ten minutes ago. Said your cell was off."

Damn. She'd forgotten to turn it back on this morning. Megan made a mental note to call Clay. Then she headed back outside to see what Clover wanted. She found her employee talking with Bobby King by the café's sidewalk table. Three customers were browsing the soaps, and one was waiting to pay for blackberry jam, a five-dollar bill hanging from his hand.

"Just who I need," King said. "Can we talk."

Megan looked from King to Clover. "You'll be okay by yourself?"

Clover smiled. "I'll be fine."

"Ten minutes, Bobby. I have customers to take care of. It's a holiday, after all."

King nodded. Megan saw the stress play out in his clenched hands and rigid jaw, and she felt her own body tense.

"Your office or the canal." King shifted impatiently.

"You tell me."

King glanced around. The town center was busy, and even by the canal, small groups had gathered for picnics and to play catch. "Office."

Megan and King went around the back of the building, and Megan let them into the kitchen. When Bibi saw them together, her eyebrows shot up in question. Megan shrugged. In the office, she closed the door behind her and sat behind her desk, motioning for King to take the chair opposite.

"What's up? You look stressed for a Fourth of July."

"I'll cut right to the chase, Megan. You need to tell me how you knew the deceased, Penelope Greenleaf. *Please.* It'll save us both a lot of heartache and headaches."

"I've already told you, Bobby. I didn't know her. I saw her all of three times—at Merry's Flower Shop, in the car when she and her sisters had a flat, and then again at the restaurant. Other than those three times, I have never set eyes on the woman. Well, other than...you know."

"Never?"

"No, never."

King rubbed his temple, never taking his gaze off Megan. "Then how the hell did she know you?"

"Why are you asking me this? What's happened."

King leaned in and steepled his hands in front of his face. "We searched Penelope's belongings. As I told you before, she and her sisters were staying at the Bucks County Inn. We found...information."

"What kind of information?"

"On her computer. She had a file on you, Megan. Where you live, the café, your law career stuff, even information about Mick," he looked pointedly at Megan, "including his obituary."

"Like Ryan found at the Marshall house." Megan shut her eyes, opened them. She felt a stabbing pain behind her left temple. "Why the obituary? Why Mick?"

"Think about an obituary, Megan. Mick died while you both lived in Chicago, but he was buried in Winsome. Someone looking for you could find information. Hometown. Names of family members."

"Why would someone want that?"

King was silent. He pulled a notebook and pen out of his shirt pocket. "This is where we get official."

Again, Megan went through the order of events: the nursery, the rain, the flat, the interrupted dinner with Denver. "I have nothing else to tell you."

"You have absolutely no idea why this woman would be interested in you?"

"Like you said before, maybe she was writing an article on

the farm and was doing her research.'"

"She was a piano teacher."

"Maybe she thought she knew me. Maybe she wanted to start a farm. Maybe she loves obituaries. I have no clue, Bobby. You're the cop—why was this woman interested in me? When I told you I was concerned days ago, you pooh-poohed me. Now all of a sudden, it's official business."

King chewed on his bottom lip. Said nothing.

Megan pressed. "After all we've been through together, you owe me an answer."

"The sister, Olive, insists you had something to do with Penelope's death and Claire's disappearance."

"That's nonsense." When he didn't respond, Megan said more loudly, "You do know that's nonsense, right? Why would I wish them harm? I didn't even know them."

King glanced behind him, toward the door. "Look, calm down, okay? We don't need anyone hearing us. Olive says her sister seemed intently focused on you. Not your farm, not Winsome, not Bonnie—you. She had some kind of dirt or something on you. She's insinuating that you killed her to keep her quiet."

"Insinuating or accusing?"

King looked down at the table, fiddled with his watch.

Megan's breath was coming faster now. "None of this is true. What dirt would anyone have on me?" She slammed a hand down on the desk. "Shame on you, Bobby King. You should know me better than this."

King rubbed his temples, avoiding eye contact. "Look, you give me some alibi information, I make an official report, and we move on. But she's making accusations, and I have to be honest, the stuff on her sister's computer backs her up."

"It only backs up that her sister was interested in me for

some reason, a reason Olive may know. Olive may be trying to shift attention by projecting a motive on to me. I'm telling you: I had nothing to do with any of this."

"The coroner believes Penelope was murdered on Thursday morning between the hours of nine and noon. She says she was strangled somewhere else, and her body was transported to the Marshall property. Can you tell me where you were Thursday morning?"

"Of course I can. I was right here—and I was with you for a portion of that time. Remember? You came to talk to me about Duke."

King's face remained impassive. He jotted something in his notebook. "What time did you arrive at the café that day?"

"Early. Probably eight or eight thirty. Clay and Porter had the farm locked down, so I stayed here to do paperwork. Alvaro can vouch for me. Then Merry stopped by, and after Merry, you came calling." Megan folded her arms across her chest. "That alibi enough for you, Bobby?"

Bobby's face had turned crimson. "That'll do."

"I can't believe you even entertained the thought that I could have killed that woman."

"I have to be objective. You're a lawyer, you know that's how the law works."

"Was a lawyer, and some of the ethical gymnastics I had to do...no thank you."

King rose.

"Not so fast," Megan said. "Since you're here, I need to talk to you. It's about Claire von Tressler."

"I can't, Megan. I need to write this up. The fact that you were in her computer makes me nervous. You were right about it being personal. I don't like it, and we need to figure out what the connection is."

"Olive has come to the Marshall house multiple times. Plus, we went to Philadelphia last night, and—"

But King had already opened the door. "I'll try to swing by later and we can talk, okay? Until then, if Olive returns, call the station. Will you do that?"

He left before Megan could answer.

Fourteen

Still seething, Megan closed the door to her office after King left. She was feeling shaken, not just because Olive was making accusations about her—that was bad enough—but because Penny had been keeping a file on her. Why? Had she been stalking her? Had she planned to blackmail her, or hurt her, or worse—hurt someone she loved? And who had killed Penny? Had that person been involved in whatever schemes Penny Greenleaf had been cooking up? Could this somehow be linked to Mick?

Megan doubted that Penny's body being on her property was a coincidence. She was beginning to doubt that the flat tire the sisters had was accidental, or that anything anyone in that extended family had told her was true.

She could hear Alvaro and Bibi chatting in the kitchen. She could hear the muted sounds of a town celebrating: horns and megaphones and an occasional excited scream. I should be out there, she thought, but there is no way I'm letting that woman or anyone connected to the von Tresslers mess with me, Bibi, or the life we've built for ourselves.

Megan booted up her office laptop. She had no idea what she was looking for—she just wanted something, anything that could connect her to that family. She opened a search engine and tried different combinations. Her name and Penelope's name. Her name and 'von Trerssler.' Even Mick's name and the von Tressler names. Nothing.

A search on Olive gave up a few social media pages with privacy locked tight, an old 5K running time, and a LinkedIn page that was virtually devoid of relevant information. Penny's online presence was only slightly better. Social media listed her as divorced, and her LinkedIn page noted several music teaching jobs. Megan repeated the exercise with Claire—nothing worthwhile to show for it.

Megan threw her head back in frustration. She knew this was fruitless. She didn't have King's resources, she didn't know where to start.

Start at the beginning. It was Mick's voice that echoed in her brain. When Megan had been a new, nervous associate at one of Chicago's largest law firms, she'd get tapped for depositions. She worked for a defense firm, and she'd spent endless hours coming up with questions to ask the plaintiffs about their accusations. When she was frustrated or at a standstill in her preparations, Mick would always tell her to start at the beginning. Who was the first person to make the allegation? What was the first thing that happened? Follow that trail.

It was good advice. Mick always had good advice.

Megan glanced at the small bookshelf against the far wall of her storage-room-turned-office. Amongst the cookbooks and business treatises was a lone picture of Mick Sawyer in uniform. Tall, trim, strikingly handsome, kind. She closed her eyes. So many emotions threatened to overwhelm her. Longing, grief, regret, guilt.

Guilt. She was alive, and he wasn't. She was here with another man. A man she loved. Not the hot-burning, can't-live-without-you kind of love she had felt for Mick when they were young, but a slow burning kind of love, one that carried a ferocity of its own.

I would want it that way, Megan. I don't want you to be alone.

Mick's voice again, or her own wishful thinking?

A knock at the door interrupted her thoughts. "Come in," she called.

It was Bibi carrying a plate of doughnuts and a coffee. "I saw Bobby leave. Thought you may need some refreshments." She placed the offerings on the desk before closing the door and sitting in the seat King had vacated. "What did he want?"

Megan hesitated, remembered their discussion earlier, and told Bibi everything.

"She actually accused you of murder?"

"Sounds that way."

"Bobby actually entertained it?"

"He was doing his job."

"Bull-cocky." Bibi waved her hand. "That boy should know better. I have a mind to call his mother. She's the one person who he will listen to."

Megan smiled, despite the tension. "Bibi, don't make me regretting telling you. We can't fix this with a call to Ann King."

"Humph."

"Do you know these people at all? Can you think of any reason Penny Greenleaf might have had an interest in me or Mick? In you?"

Bibi shook her head. Alvaro called from the other room.

"I should go. He's making tortillas and doughnuts. Soon someone will have a taco with cinnamon and sugar on it. Or worse, a donut stuffed with fish."

"Go, Bibi. He needs you."

Bibi frowned. "You're not going to sit here and stew all day, are you?"

At that moment, Megan decided she was not going to do that at all. "In fact, I'm headed out there shortly," she said.

"Good. I love you, you know."

Megan smiled. "I love you, too."

She watched her grandmother leave, her gait a little slow and stiff this morning. *Start from the beginning.* With a heavy but determined heart, she returned to the computer. She had one more thing to look up before she'd head out of this room and back into the world.

Von Tressler Investments had its headquarters on Arch Street in Philadelphia. Megan found the phone number and dialed. A receptionist answered.

"Dominick von Tressler, please."

"I'm afraid Mr. von Tressler's not in today. May I take a message?"

"Do you expect him tomorrow?"

"I really can't say, Ms.—"

"Megan Sawyer," Megan said. "I'll try him again tomorrow."

Putting the phone back in its cradle, Megan thought about the von Tressler family. A father who started a multi-million-dollar business. A son and a wife who betrayed and humiliated him. A nephew who was given control. A wronged wife. An abandoned mansion. Lots of motives for murder there. Revenge. Greed. Rage. The only problem was, the person who was dead—Penny—seemed removed from all of it.

Penelope Greenleaf, piano teacher, sister of Martin von Tressler's wife. Who would want Penny dead? Could it have been a random murder after all? No...the flowers, the timing. Or was she skipping over some vital connection that would cause all of this to make sense?

Megan put away her laptop and grabbed her purse. She'd

check on the sidewalk sale and then head out. The Bucks County Inn. She hadn't been there in a while. After the deaths the year before, she'd hoped never to go again.

Fifteen

The Bucks County Inn was a stately Colonial on a picturesque property. Situated a few miles outside of Winsome, it was a favorite with visitors because it was close enough to be convenient to the city and New Hope, but it offered elegant, high-end accommodations. The proprietor, an older woman with a penchant for all things Scottish, knew Megan, and she and her dog, a Scottish Terrier, greeted her warmly when Megan arrived.

"Olive Dunkel?" The woman looked through a registry on her desk. "Yes, yes. I don't know that she's here now, though. Shall I call her room, dear?"

"If you don't mind."

Megan waited while the innkeeper made the call. She hung up after a few rings.

"I don't think her car is out there, Megan. I believe she's gone somewhere."

The dog rubbed her head against Megan's leg. She bent to pet its head. "Can you give her a message?"

The proprietor handed her a square of notepaper with a Scottish flag in the corner. Megan was in the middle of writing her name and a message on the paper when the front door opened. She turned her head to see Olive Dunkel wedging her way inside. Olive didn't notice her at first. She walked past the reception desk obliviously until the proprietor cleared her throat.

"Olive?"

Olive stopped mid-stride. She was carrying two Whole Foods reusable bags that seemed to be filled with clothes. Her red hair looked unkempt and unwashed, her face devoid of make-up. Unlike the first day Megan saw her, when she was dolled up from head to toe in Donna Karan, today she wore ill-fitting jeans and an oversized sequined t-shirt.

"Megan," she said, "why are you here?"

"I'd like to talk to you."

Olive looked at Megan, then the proprietor, and then back at Megan. She swallowed repeatedly. Finally she nodded. "Give me ten minutes to shower and change."

"Do you want some lunch, dear?" the proprietor called after her.

If Olive heard, she didn't respond.

"Let's go outside," Megan said. She led Olive, who looked better after her shower and a change into a black velour track suit, out to the patio, where several umbrella-topped tables had been set up.

The innkeeper had already set out a pitcher of iced tea, two glasses, and a plate of sugar cookies. Megan poured each of them some tea.

"Why are you here?" Olive asked again. Her gaze never strayed from the glass of iced tea. "Is this about my sister?"

"I don't know what makes you think I had anything to do with your sister's death, but I can assure you, I didn't know Penny. I had never set eyes on your sister until the day the three of you walked into Merry's Flowers. I've already spoken to the police. In fact, I was at the café and talking to the Chief when your sister was...well, during the relevant time."

"First Claire, then Penny."

"I know. I don't understand it, either." Megan leaned down in an attempt make Olive look into her eyes. "There is some reason why your sister was focused on me, and I'd like to know what it was as much as you would."

Tears rolled down Olive's cheeks. "I want my sister back."

"I know you do."

"I came here with two sisters, and I'm leaving with none."

"Claire is still alive. You have to believe that."

Olive gulped, eyes still moist. She took a sip of the tea, wiped her mouth with a cloth napkin, and shook her head. "I don't. In my gut, I believe my sister is dead."

Megan sat silently, letting Olive cry. A cardinal landed on a bird feeder that hung from a post at the far end of the patio. Megan watched its head bobble back and forth before it pecked at the food. Olive sobbed, and the bird flew away.

"Why are you here, Megan?" Olive asked again softly.

"You've come to the farm several times. You were with your sister the night before she was killed." *Start at the beginning.* "You know the von Tressler family."

"So?"

"So, we can help each other."

Olive wiped her eyes daintily with the corner of the same napkin. "I don't share that belief."

"Your family came here for a memorial service. Almost everything that happened seems somehow connected to that memorial. Help me understand the connection."

"Even if I wanted to help you, how do I know you're not just trying to shift blame elsewhere?"

"What do I gain by doing that? The police have already

questioned me. They know I have an alibi. If I really had something to hide, something that your sister could use against me, do you think I would be actively trying to determine what it was—and asking for your help in the process?"

Olive's shoulders slumped. She shook her head slowly back and forth.

"I just need some answers, that's all. Answers only you can provide."

Olive sat up straight. She seemed to teeter on the brink of saying something for a moment before standing up and looking around. "If we're going to talk, I need a real drink."

"Tell me about Martin von Tressler," Megan said.

"Well that's quite an open-ended question." Megan waited while the other woman downed half her drink in two swallows. "Martin, huh? He was what they called in the old days a 'cad.'"

"A womanizer?"

"Oh, it was more than that. He was charming and charismatic and someone women *wanted* to be around." Olive smiled. It was a pretty smile, and it made her look a decade younger. "I should know. I met Martin first."

Megan's eyes widened. "Claire met him through you?"

"She sure did. I worked for von Tressler Furniture out of college. I moved up through the ranks, eventually becoming a regional manager. One year I won an award. The celebration was held at the Four Seasons, high society back then, and the President of the company personally congratulated me. We started talking, he said he was looking for a personal assistant at his home in Chestnut Hill, and I suggested my younger sister, who was once again underemployed."

"And he hired her."

"Not at first. He found someone else, later fired her, and called me to inquire about Claire. Claire was working part-time at a tailor shop, and she jumped at the chance to move up the ladder, as she called it." Olive smiled, clearly remembering. "I remember the first time Martin saw her. He was in his seventies already, but he was still trim and handsome and sharp. He had a thing for games. Would tease Claire, then back off. When he decided he wanted her, he pulled out all the stops."

"He swept Claire off her feet?"

"He bribed her into loving him, if you could call it love."

"Was it immediate?"

"Gosh, no. The years she worked for him, and it was years, he bought her jewelry and chocolates, and gave her a credit card to use on her own purchases. We grew up pretty poor. My father was blue collar, and I told you he died young, when Claire was still a kid. My mother tried her best by piecing together sewing jobs and teaching at the local Catholic school, but it never seemed to be enough." She stared at her glass wistfully. "It was Penny who felt the brunt of it because she was sent to work instead of school."

Megan ran a finger around the rim of her glass. A picture was emerging, one of a poor family and girl who would do anything to escape that poverty. "So Claire was ripe for the attention?"

"Ripe for a lot of things. Tired of the teasing and the games, Martin finally proposed, and she accepted. We had a huge wedding—you'd never know Claire was his fourth wife—and things went south from there."

The inn's proprietor stuck her head outside to see if Megan and Olive wanted anything. Olive held up her glass and asked for another gin and tonic.

"What was I saying?"

"Things went south."

"Yes! And did they. We watched from afar as Claire screwed everything up. She finally had the nice house and the fancy clothes and the expensive cars and, perhaps most of all, the respect she wanted, but she threw it all in the trash along with her reputation."

"David?"

"He wasn't the first."

Megan's eyebrows shot up in surprise.

"Don't look so shocked. She may seem like an innocent, all mopey over her lost love, but Claire is more complicated than that." Olive tilted her head and smiled. "You look shocked again. Is it because I'm bad mouthing the sister I'm desperate to find? You know what true love is, Megan? It's loving someone despite their faults. I love my sisters—both of them—in spite of the dumb things they've done."

"Claire had cheated on Martin before David. Did Martin know?"

"To Claire's credit, she never really pretended to love Martin. He was in his eighties when he died, she had just turned thirty. It was a summer-winter romance, and like all things in summer, Claire was sowing her oats. Martin's days of sowing anything without medicinal help were mostly over. He had a litany of health problems. Couldn't travel, couldn't tolerate rich foods, didn't like crowds. The one thing he still liked, though, was Claire."

"So she played along."

The innkeeper returned with another drink. Olive thanked her, took a sip, and sighed. "No. She never really had to. As long as she kept her boy toys discreet, and as long as she did the things he asked of her, some of which, frankly, were on the kinky side, he was happy. I don't think Martin was any more capable of love in that relationship than she was."

"Control."

"Right. When you have a massage, you want the therapist to pay attention to you. You want to feel relaxed and special for that hour. You're not asking for her to love you, you don't care that she has other clients, as long as she's there when you need her."

"You want your money's worth."

This time it was Olive who looked surprised. "A very coarse way of saying it, but yes. He wanted his money's worth." Another sip, followed by a deep swig. "When she hooked up with David, everything changed."

"Too personal?"

"David was just like his father, except in an improved form. Fitter, sharper, more emotionally available. Not perfect, mind you. Still narcissistic as only the very rich or powerful can be. But he and Claire had something very akin to love."

Megan recalled the David she'd met a few times. Slender, elegant. Always dressed in a tailored suit, always smelling of expensive aftershave. Violet eyes, a weak chin saved by facial hair. Not her type, but she could see the attraction. Megan looked up to see Olive staring at her.

"I don't see how any of this walk down memory lane is helpful," Olive said.

"It is. Please, go on."

"There is little else. The affair between my sister and David spanned months, maybe years—who knows. When Melanie found out, she hit the roof. It was she who called Martin. By then, everyone at work knew, and livid Martin stripped David of his role. Gave it to that upstart, Dominick, instead."

Questions queued in Megan's head. She started with, "How could he strip David of his role if David was an owner of the business?"

"Smart girl. Martin was still head of the non-public company. The board owed him, and each member knew it. His son was promised half of the business, but he never had anything in writing. A generous salary, expensive car, expense account. All the accoutrements of an owner without the actual shares."

Things were starting to make sense. "So when he was banished, that was it. He had no leverage when trying to fight his demotion."

"Exactly."

"Melanie stayed with him anyway."

"Obviously. Oh, she was angry. Threatened my sister, threatened to leave David, but in the end, she stayed."

"Money talks?"

Olive shrugged. "I couldn't begin to guess."

"How did Martin die?"

"He had a stroke in his sleep. Never woke up."

"There were issues between David, Melanie, and Claire. Issues related to Martin's will? You suggested it when we saw each other at the farmers market."

Olive didn't answer at first. Then, "I don't really know about that."

Megan watched as the innkeeper made her way across the patio with an armful of fluffy white towels. The inn had a small pool at the very rear of the property, and the excited cries of children could be heard from across the fence. Olive turned in the direction of the pool and frowned.

"Happy sounds," Megan said.

"Impossible to nap here. Kids playing all day long. You try relaxing with so many kids around."

"Try relaxing with goats, chickens, dogs, and a spirited

grandmother."

Olive cracked a smile. "Touché."

They sat quietly for a moment before Olive drained her glass and slapped a hand down on the table. She started to rise. "Speaking of naps, I'm tired."

"One more question, Olive."

Olive settled back onto the edge of her seat. "What?"

"Where is Claire living now?"

"I have no idea," Olive said. "She's disappeared on us."

"What I mean is, before she disappeared, where was she living. Is she still in the house she shared with Martin?"

Olive looked as though she'd refuse to answer. Her thin, wide lips set into a frown, and her eyes narrowed. "It's a big house."

"That's why I'm wondering."

"Martin could be vindictive. My sister chose not to stay there. She was staying with my brother, in New Jersey."

"Why not with you or Penny?"

Olive stood up. She drained some liquid that had melted into her glass, picked up three cookies and placed them into a napkin. "Have a good afternoon, Megan. I hope you have some time to enjoy the holiday."

Megan had forgotten about the holiday. She had forgotten about the sidewalk sale and the grand opening of the barn. She could only focus on the information Olive had shared, information she wanted to corroborate as soon as possible.

Megan stood as well. She grabbed her purse and followed Olive back into the main portion of the inn. Once inside, Olive started up the stairs without another word. The innkeeper's dog rubbed herself against Megan's leg in greeting.

When Olive was upstairs and out of earshot, the innkeeper scrunched up her features. "Think that one is dramatic, you should have met the sister."

Megan smiled. "Penny? I did meet her."

"Not Penny, the other one. Younger, cute, but *clearly* emotional. I closed out her room when she failed to show for three nights straight. Her sister paid the bill."

"That was nice."

Another disgusted look. "Nice? I shouldn't speak ill of my clients, but I'm not sure 'nice' is a word I'd use to describe any of them."

Sixteen

It was after five when Megan finally got back to the farm. Bibi was still at the café, and Porter and Clay were in town as well, so she had the place to herself. After greeting Sadie and Gunther—Porter must have taken Sarge—Megan changed from her dress into shorts, a tank top, and sneakers. She made the rounds to check on the animals, Gunther by her side.

The place seemed empty and still. Even the goats, normally playful this time of day, seemed subdued, and the chickens were mostly sleeping. Gunther curled in the goat pen next to Dimples and gave Megan a look that said he wasn't leaving—for now at least. She gave him a pat and let him be.

The Marshall place was empty, too. Ryan had gone, and the house stood dark and quiet.

Not what I'm used to, Megan thought. She felt like she should work in the fields. There was so much that needed to be done: weeding and watering and planting new seeds in the greenhouse. The problem was, she didn't want to do any of those things. She wanted to make a sandwich and veg in front of the television. Or read a good book.

Or maybe a bath and a book.

Or a sandwich, a bath, and a book.

And Denver.

Megan dialed his cell phone number. He picked up

immediately, but he sounded out of breath.

"I have a rare evening alone at the farm," Megan said. "Thought maybe you'd like to come over for dinner, but it sounds like you're in the middle of something."

"Birthing a foal, Megs. Well, the horse is, not me. The lassie is having a tough time of it. Not sure when I'll be done."

"No worries. Call me later." Megan hung up, disappointed. While they always had Denver's house, which he shared with five rescue dogs, she liked having him here, in her home. But she understood. A bath, then, she thought.

She made herself two tomato and mayonnaise sandwiches on Bibi's honey wheat bread, poured an iced tea, and went upstairs, Sadie in tow. While the old clawfoot tub filled, she ate the sandwiches and watched the news. Nothing about the von Tresslers. No word on Penny's death other than a blurb in the local papers a few days ago. For that matter, very little about David's heart attack, either.

Megan looked up Dominick von Tressler. He was listed as the President and CEO of von Tressler Investments. She found his LinkedIn page and stared at the photo. This picture was recent, and showed a dark-haired man with closely-cropped hair and a suggestion of sideburns. Handsome in a nondescript way, his smile was perfunctory and bland. Despite the professional photo, Megan was sure it was the young man she'd seen with Melanie and David in town. The guy she thought had been David's son. He looked a lot like his uncle.

She scanned the LinkedIn profile. Drexel undergraduate, Wharton MBA. Worked for the von Tressler companies as an intern—and then for his entire adult life thereafter. Based on his graduation date from college, assuming he was about twenty-two when he left his undergraduate program, he was only about twenty-nine now. Young to be a CEO of such a large company, begging the question: Was Dominick a business genius/protégé, or was his appointment indicative of just how angry Martin von Tressler had been over his son's betrayal?

She needed to talk with Dominick.

Megan gave the last of her bread to Sadie, crumpled her napkin, grabbed the thriller she was reading, and walked into her bathroom to turn off the spigot. The tub was nearly full of steamy water, and she glanced at it longingly. Her back ached from lifting bins of vegetables and bales of hay, something that happened more and more frequently. I need a vacation, she thought. She stripped out of her clothes and sank into the tub.

Three pages into the chapter, she put the book down. She couldn't concentrate.

Megan went back over her conversation with Olive. She had painted Claire as an opportunist, someone who married for money without regard to feelings or true emotional connections. Yet the Claire Megan had driven to the memorial seemed genuinely devastated by David's death. Had the affair between the two been over? Was it possible she had still been seeing David behind Melanie's back?

Megan's mind flitted to her conversation with Melanie. The way Melanie recounted David's affair with Claire and the subsequent reversal of his fortune. Melanie had painted Claire in a different light—as a naïve young woman obsessed with a man who didn't love her back. Truth? Or what she wanted to believe?

And after the affair and Martin's subsequent death, had David inherited Martin's portion of the company? Or did that go to Claire? Or maybe everything went to Dominick.

All roads led to Dominick. Dominick, who seemed chummy with Melanie and her husband. Dominick, who by a twist of fate ended up as the head of a prominent Philadelphia company in his twenties. Why had Dominick been in Winsome? Just family time? Somehow Megan doubted that. Had David been planning to return to von Tressler Investments and they were negotiating terms?

Megan closed her eyes and let the warmth run over her. *Start at the beginning.* In this case, the beginning was the memorial service. Claire had been there—at least she'd arrived at the reception. Melanie had been there. Penny and Olive had arrived eventually. Had Dominick been there? Seems likely.

She couldn't talk to Claire or Penny. She had already spoken with Melanie and Olive. Who else did she know? Surely, some folks from Winsome had been employed at the von Tressler house that day. Maybe she could find out who they were.

And Merry. She had been there too. No one liked to share as much as Merry.

Megan pulled herself up and out of the tub. She toweled herself off quickly and threw on jeans and a long-sleeved light linen shirt. A glance out the window told her the evening was still clear and breezy. A perfect night to be outside.

Megan knew exactly where to find Merry later this evening. Seems like maybe she'd see the fireworks after all.

The best laid plans, Megan thought. As she sat in her truck, ready to pull out of the driveway, another car pulled in. She recognized her Aunt Sarah's vehicle, and as it moved closer, she saw Bibi in the passenger seat. Sarah and Bibi were chatting happily, so Megan wasn't worried—but she *was* curious as to why Bibi hadn't taken her own car home.

"Megan! You look wonderful." Sarah kissed Megan through the truck's window. "Are you leaving? I was hoping we could chat."

"I figured my grandmother was staying in town for the fireworks, so I thought I'd head to Canal Street. She opted not to go?"

"I'll let her tell you," Aunt Sarah said. More quietly, she whispered, "I think she's tired."

Megan's Aunt Sarah was her late grandfather's younger sister. The relationship between Bibi and Sarah had been strained for many years, but recently they'd gotten over old resentments enough to forge a new, tepid relationship. Tepid was better than tumultuous. Megan was surprised to see them together.

Sarah lived in a restored cottage on the outskirts of town. A famous mystery author who wrote under several pen names, Sarah Birch could be as elusive and reserved as some of her main characters. Megan had her own baggage when it came to her Aunt Sarah, and like most times when they were together, seeing her brought with it an onrush of feelings—not all of them pleasant.

Bibi unlocked the porch door that led into the kitchen, flipped on the light, and said "hello" to Sadie. From her vantage point in the driveway, Megan could see her grandmother shuffling around the kitchen, making herbal tea.

"Tired, huh?" Megan said. "Well, she worked on her feet all day. That would make anyone tired."

"Don't you think it's too much for her?" Aunt Sarah pursed her lips into a frown and flipped her ropey gray hair over her shoulder. A handsome woman, she carried herself with confidence and more than a hint of bravado. She was Bibi's junior by about fifteen years, but it always seemed like Bibi and Aunt Sarah had been raised in different worlds and different eras.

"The café? She loves it."

"Which is the reason she won't quit until someone makes her."

Megan refused to have this conversation with Sarah. She knew Bibi would resent her talking behind her back, and after Bibi's plea that Megan not treat her differently, Megan had resolved to be more open.

"I'll talk with her, Aunt Sarah, but it's her decision."

"But—"

Megan shook her head. "Is that the only reason why you wanted to talk with me?"

"No, actually." Aunt Sarah glanced toward the house. "It looks like Bonnie is making tea. Why don't we go inside and have some? We can talk there." Seeming to remember that Megan was on her way out, she said quickly, "I mean if you don't mind staying a little longer."

"I had been hoping to catch Merry in town. Did you see her?"

"She was there. She had a table at the sidewalk sale and was unhappy with sales. You're better off not seeing her tonight. Gripe, gripe, gripe."

Megan smiled. Sounded like Merry. She reached back into her bag for her truck keys. Griping or no griping, she would go to the fireworks and look for Merry. Whatever Aunt Sarah wanted to discuss could wait.

"There was someone asking about you, and I wanted to let you know in person." Aunt Sarah eyed the keys Megan was now holding. "Fifteen minutes?"

She had Megan's attention. "Fifteen minutes."

Inside, Bibi was already sitting at the kitchen table, mug of tea in front of her alongside a plate of banana bread slices. She was digging into a slice of banana bread and had a second piece on her plate.

"Aren't you supposed to watch your sugar?" Aunt Sarah asked.

"Aren't you supposed to mind your business?" Bibi flashed a half smile, but her *back off* message was clear.

Megan poured Aunt Sarah and herself tea and joined them at the table.

"Where's your car?" she asked her grandmother.

"I have a flat tire."

"Really? Those are new tires." Megan always put snow tires on her grandmother's car in winter and all season tires back on in the spring. "Did you run over something?"

"It looked questionable," Aunt Sarah said. "We called the police."

"Why would someone slash your tires?" Megan said.

"Tire," Bibi responded. "Just one."

"What did the cops say?" Megan asked.

"We didn't wait for them. They were apparently busy." Bibi sipped her tea and took another bite of bread. Megan could tell by the way she eyed the plate that she was debating a third slice.

"They said they would come by when they could," Aunt Sarah said. "I guess with the Fourth of July festivities plus whatever else nonsense people do on holiday weekends— drinking and driving and such—a flat was low on their list."

As though on cue, sirens wailed in the distance. "You probably should have waited to give a statement."

"I didn't feel like waiting," Bibi snapped. "I was ready to go home."

Megan studied her grandmother. Bibi looked tired: bags under her eyes, skin a little pale, shoulders not quite as pin-straight as usual. Maybe Aunt Sarah was right and this was too much for her.

"Tell her about that woman," Bibi said to Aunt Sarah.

"Right." She turned toward Megan. "You know the woman who died on the old Marshall property?"

"Penny Greenleaf."

"Yes, her. She asked to speak with me two days before she died. She had found out that I'm your aunt, and she wanted to know about you—where you live, how long you've lived here, etc."

Megan wasn't surprised given what King had told her, but she was surprised that Penny had found out Sarah was her aunt. That wasn't common knowledge outside the Winsome circle. Megan said as much to Aunt Sarah.

"I was surprised, too, and frankly rather taken aback."

"Did she say why she wanted to know about me?"

"No, she didn't. She seemed very focused on you, though, and was annoyingly insistent with her questions."

"What did you tell her?"

Bibi and Aunt Sarah exchanged a glance.

"To talk to you herself," Aunt Sarah said.

Megan could feel a headache creeping around the edges of her skull. Penelope Greenleaf—what the hell did she want with me, Megan thought.

"Does her name ring a bell to you?" Bibi asked Aunt Sarah. "Maybe an old relative or family friend?"

Aunt Sarah shook her head. "Never heard of her before. She said she was a distant relative of the von Tresslers. Do you know if that's right?"

Megan told her aunt the little she knew about Penny. "Why she was interested in me remains a mystery."

"Someone knows," Aunt Sarah said.

"What do you mean?" Bibi asked.

"Penny's body was found on Megan's property. I'm sure

that wasn't a coincidence."

Someone...but who? Megan felt the tension headache growing and throbbing, tightening like a vise around her temples. She rose to find some pain reliever, which Bibi usually kept in the cabinet over the sink.

"If you had to guess, would you say Penny was asking questions in order to blackmail me about something? That's what her sister seems to think."

Sarah seemed to consider this. While she waited for a response, Megan sifted through the pill bottles to find the Tylenol. She saw it, grabbed the bottle, and was about to pull it out when her attention settled on the other pill bottles in the cabinet. Prescription painkillers with Bibi's name on them. Prescriptions Megan didn't know about. She closed the door, took her Tylenol, and sat back down, wondering again whether Bibi was being fully honest with *her*.

"So what do you think?" she asked her aunt. "Nefarious intent?"

"She told me she was interested in your work. I neither believed nor disbelieved her. I don't think she was up to something illegal, but she is dead, so I supposed there may have been more than meets the eye."

Aunt Sarah spoke with her usual matter-of-fact tone, but Megan thought she could hear the tiniest bit of worry. If unflappable Sarah Birch was worried, that worried Megan even more. And now the tire on Bibi's car. Sinister—or coincidence?

"She did say something that made me like her a little. She was a huge mystery fan. Rattled off all the greats."

"Including yours?" Bibi asked without a trace of irony.

Sarah threw her head back and laughed. "She'd read every one of my books. Said she and her brother were huge fans."

Her brother, Megan thought. The same brother who had

been living with Claire? "Did she mention this brother's name?"

Aunt Sarah drummed her fingers on the tabletop. "Hmmm...yes, she did, I think. Said he was a writer, too, and had I heard of him. First name Ethan or Evan or something like that. Last name James."

Ethan or Evan James from New Jersey. Someone else who might know where Claire was.

"I'm pretty certain it's Evan." Aunt Sarah nodded emphatically. "Yes, Evan."

"Thank you," Megan said.

"For what?"

"For stopping by." She kissed her grandmother and aunt on the head and grabbed her purse. It was not too late to find Merry in town. Her phone rang and she glanced at it. Denver. She answered. "Yes?"

"Still at the farm, Megs?"

"I am."

"Still alone?" Voice a shade huskier.

"No."

"Darn. But I can still come by?"

Megan dropped her purse. Fireworks and Merry were not meant to happen. "I would love that."

"Give me thirty to shower and change. Tell Bibi I'll pick up some Ben & Jerry's on the way."

Megan glanced at her grandmother, who was nearly finished with her third slice of banana bread. "Don't worry about stopping," she said. "Bibi is sweet enough."

Seventeen

By midday Tuesday, the temperatures and humidity felt oppressive, which was especially unpleasant after the beautiful holiday Mother Nature had granted. Megan took the weather in stride—it was part of farming after all—but Bibi wasn't quite as serene. Megan found her in the parlor with their small window air conditioner turned up to full blast and a fan on.

"Hot?" Megan asked. She'd just returned from the greenhouse, and her fingernails were caked with dirt. "I can get you a cold iced tea. Let me wash up."

"I think I might need to *bathe* in cold iced tea. What is it? A hundred and twenty degrees out there?"

"Ninety-four with a hundred percent humidity."

"It's like swimming in a vat of sweat."

Megan laughed. Her grandmother was right. "I'm heading to Merry's. Need anything?"

"Some more potting soil? I want to transplant a few of the house plants later, when it's cooler."

Megan agreed—it would give her a good excuse to be at Merry's, anyway. She considered asking Bibi about the painkiller prescriptions but decided to wait. Bibi seemed in a good mood. She didn't want to ruin it.

"I may be gone a while. I have a few other errands to make."

Bibi's mouth twisted. "Do you think you can let Alvaro

know I'll be late today? I may just go over for a few hours in the afternoon."

Megan paused by the door. "Tuesdays are pretty slow, Bibi. I'm sure he'll manage if you'd prefer to stay here. Yesterday was a busy day for you."

"It's not because I'm tired. Emily's picking me up. She can't get here until one."

Bibi's car. Megan had completely forgotten. "Yes, I'll tell him. Shall I call the garage to see if they can get your car?"

"Already done. I also spoke to King. He said a police report was drafted. He wants you to call him, by the way. And so does Clay. You never called him back.

Forgetful, back aches...I'm the one slipping, not Bibi, Megan thought. "Will do. See you later. Call me if anything comes up."

Outside, the heat was stifling. The house had no central air, but at least the window air conditioners and the deep stone sills kept the interior moderately cool. Megan started the truck and turned the air on high. As she pulled out of the driveway, she called Clay, who was off today. No answer. Next, she rang King. He answered on the fourth ring.

"Megan, I'm glad you called. Did Bibi tell you about her car?"

"She sure did. Accident?"

"Probably. Looks like she drove over something sharp."

"May be worth looking into another flat."

"You mean the sisters' flat the day of the memorial?"

"Yep. May have been a true accident, but maybe Olive would know. Or maybe she can tell you who fixed it."

"Good idea."

Megan stopped at a stop sign and waited for King to end the call. Instead, he said, "There was a break in at the von

Tressler residence last night."

"Really?"

"Yep. Melanie and her mother were in town for the festivities. Someone broke a window into the basement. Alarm was triggered, but the police found a rock with a typed note inside."

"What did it say?"

"*Get out.*"

Megan pictured the layout of the house. "Did the person throw it through the back window or around front?"

"The back. Why?"

"Just curious. The place seemed like Fort Knox. Seems odd that someone would make it to the back of that huge property, have time to throw the rock, and leave the hillside before the alarm was triggered and the cops arrived."

"There are trees all around, and it was dark out. They could have hidden in the woods. Plus, whoever it was took advantage of the fireworks. The town and the police were distracted."

"True." Megan realized he wasn't telling her this for nothing. "Why are you letting me know?"

"Because Melanie thinks whoever did this is tied to Penny's death. She and her mother are convinced that the same person is after Melanie. If that's true—"

"They may be after me, too."

"Right." He paused. "Penny's body was on your property."

Megan rubbed her temples. It's not as though she hadn't thought of it herself, of course. But the fact that it happened yesterday means that if Melanie was right, the person responsible was still in Winsome.

King asked, "Did anything odd happen at the farm? Anymore Olive visits or papers left behind."

"Not that I'm aware of. Just Bibi's car."

King was silent. Then, "Be careful, Megan."

"Before you get off the line, Olive mentioned that before her disappearance, Claire had been staying with her older brother, a man named Evan James. Have you talked to him?"

"We have. Kind of a deadbeat. Has a record of his own. Theft, possession—petty stuff. Been in prison a few times. Not very helpful when it came to Claire."

"I looked him up. He says he's a writer. Didn't mention Claire, but his writing was very stream-of-consciousness stuff. Maybe that's how he processes. Did you talk to him in person?"

Another voice came through the phone. King being paged.

"I have to go, Megan. And no, we didn't talk to him in person. Between the murder and Claire's disappearance, we're spread pretty thin. Talked to him, he had an alibi and no clue where his sister is." More static-y voices through the line. "I'll catch up with you later."

Megan hung up. At a stop sign, she glanced down at the paper on the passenger seat. Evan James, forty-four years old, Flemington, New Jersey.

First Merry, then a road trip to New Jersey. Maybe she'd pick up a few clues along the way.

Merry's Flowers was unusually busy, and once again Megan found herself waiting in line to pay. When the checkout counter was finally empty, Megan approached. She put Bibi's potting soil and a pair of gardening gloves on the counter.

"We missed you last night," Merry said, looking at Megan over aquamarine readers that matched a plaid aquamarine and navy checked dress. "Everyone was at the fireworks. Well, almost everyone."

"I tried to go, but we had visitors."

Merry flashed her a knowing smile. "That handsome boyfriend of yours?"

"Eventually. Before that, Aunt Sarah."

Merry let out a dramatic sigh. "Sarah and I used to walk two miles every other day. Now she's facing a deadline and it's excuse after excuse." She glanced at the register and announced the price. "Cash or credit?"

Megan handed her a twenty. While Merry made change, Megan switched the subject to the memorial. "How was it? Bobby King told me you made it over."

"Oh, that? Yes, I figured someone should be there to represent the town. Roger was busy, so I went alone."

"How was it?"

Raised, heavily tweezed eyebrows gave Merry's face a comical look. "Now you're curious?"

"I spoke to Melanie a few days ago. She said it was well attended." A lie, but Megan figured Merry would take the bait.

"Is that what Melanie said? Perhaps to her that was a big crowd. A bunch of corporate types, some wannabe socialites, and those sisters."

"Yes, Melanie mentioned that they were there."

Merry nodded. "All but the youngest. But you know that—you supposedly dropped her off."

"Supposedly?" Megan wasn't sure whether to laugh or be offended. "Next you'll say I allegedly kidnapped her."

Merry's combination of an eyeroll and shoulder shrug proclaimed that anything could happen.

"Melanie said you were chatting with the sisters." Another fib, but Merry was annoying her, so she decided to go all in.

"Hardly. I spoke to them for a few minutes, tops. The blond was downright rude. Kept looking around when I spoke to her. The other one seemed more concerned with finding her sister,

Claire. It was like talking to teenage boys at a junior high dance. No focus."

"You said the blond, Penny, seemed distracted? Was she looking for Claire, too?"

"How should I know?"

"How about a young guy named Dominick von Tressler. Kind of short, wiry. David's nephew. Looks like David."

Merry's forehead creased in thought. "Maybe. I seem to recall seeing him, but I can't say for sure." Merry handed Megan her change. "Why all the questions?"

"As you noted, I dropped Claire off at that memorial. Allegedly, she never showed up. I think I have a right to ask questions."

"The police don't suspect you, do they?" Merry asked, perking up behind a façade of concern.

"No, of course not, but I can't help but feel bad." Megan pocketed the change. No one was nearby, and she leaned in. "Did Melanie seem distraught?"

"Distraught? I wouldn't say that. I really didn't see much of her. Her mother, that Veronica woman, seemed to be running the show. She greeted people at the door, kept the drinks flowing. Melanie showed up later, said her hellos, and disappeared again."

"Disappeared?"

"Into the bowels of that ghastly house."

"Did you see her with the sisters?"

"Not that I recall. My, this is like Bobby King's interrogation. Are you working for the police now?"

Megan smiled. "Merry, can you think of any Winsome people who were working there that day? Anyone who might remember something useful?"

A customer was approaching the cash register, and Merry

glanced their way. "From Winsome? I don't think so." The customer, an elderly man with a full gray beard, placed a bird feeder and some birdseed on the counter. Merry started ringing him up, dismissing Megan with a curt nod.

Megan was halfway out the door when she heard Merry say, "Jenny Clark, Roger's niece. She was serving appetizers and drinks. May want to give her a ring."

"Thanks," Megan said. She knew Jenny, a college student who was living with her uncle for the summer.

"Anything to keep you out of trouble. What would Bibi do without you?"

Eighteen

Flemington, New Jersey was a traffic-filled forty minutes from Winsome. Megan left Merry's and figured she could be in Flemington and back before anyone missed her. She followed Route 202 through Pennsylvania, over the bridge to New Jersey, and kept going. The address she had for Evan James took her to a renovated Victorian on the back side of town. Wedged between a WaWa and a service station, the house's mint green paint was peeling off the trim like curls of ribbon. The body of the house looked as though it hadn't been touched up in a decade. Three kids' bikes sat locked to a net-less basketball hoop. An old Buick sat in the driveway, one tire noticeably flat.

Megan knocked on the ground floor apartment. She could hear someone talking on the other side of the door, but it took four loud knocks before the door opened. A man in stained gray sweatpants and a once-white ribbed tank top peeked out from behind the door. Uncombed salt-and-pepper hair, three-days' worth of stubble, a cigarette hanging out of his mouth. He looked Megan up and down.

"Yeah."

"Evan James?"

"Yeah."

"My name is Megan Sawyer. I know your sister, Claire. May

I talk to you for a few minutes?"

The man took one step outside. Megan saw bright white gym socks and, above that, a band of leg about the same color.

"You gotta be friggin kidding me. This again? Are you a cop?"

"No, I'm just someone concerned about Claire's welfare."

"Claire's a big girl."

"Just a few questions."

"I'm busy working."

When Megan didn't budge, Evan's expression softened. He threw the cigarette on the ground outside and left it there. Megan stepped on it, resisting the urge to pick it up.

"Fine. Come on in. Don't mind the mess. My maid has the day off." He laughed heartily at his own joke. "Want some water? I don't drink—recovery—so I can't offer you a beer."

It was only eleven thirty in the morning, but Megan chose not to point that out. "No, thanks. I'm fine."

"How'd you find me?"

"Your sisters."

"Big mouths, all of them. Come this way."

Mess was an understatement. The door opened into a cramped kitchen. A row of cheap oak cabinets with plywood countertops lined one wall. The sink was piled with dirty dishes, and newspapers and dishes took up every inch of the counter. The stove was topped with a thick layer of grime, and on top of that, a half dozen dirty pots and frying pans. Only the refrigerator—stainless steel and smudge free—seemed clean or new.

Evan led her through the kitchen and into a dining room/living room. If it was hot outside, it was worse in here. A single fan on a side table blew warm air and cigarette smoke. The furniture consisted of a ripped loveseat, a recliner, and a

Formica-topped table littered with newspapers, magazines, and balls of crushed printer paper. A laptop sat in the middle of the mess. The place stunk of cat urine and cigarette smoke.

"My writing cave," Evan said. "Sit, please."

Megan perched on the edge of the couch. Evan sank into the recliner. He lit another cigarette. Sweat beaded along his upper lip, above his hairline. Megan could feel it trickling between her breasts and down her back.

"How do you know Claire?"

"We met in Winsome."

"Pennsylvania? Nice. I told the cops I haven't heard from her in almost two weeks. They didn't seem to believe me, so I thought maybe you were here to follow up." He threw his arms up in the air. "Look around. Her bedroom is back there," he pointed to a door that led from the living room to the rear of the apartment, "and I can assure you, the only things she left here are some old clothes and a worthless set of CDs." He shrugged bony shoulders. "Besides, the house wouldn't look like this if Claire were here. She's a neat freak. Used to a fancy life."

"I'm not with the police, and I'm not here to check up on you. I was just hoping to ask you a few questions."

"Ask away. Can't promise I'll answer."

"How long has Claire been living here?"

"I don't know. I told the cops, maybe nine months? A year? Off and on since her old man croaked."

"Why didn't she stay at the Philadelphia estate?"

"You gotta ask her. My opinion? It's a creepy place. Who'd want to stay there alone?"

Echoing Denver, Megan thought. And they were both right; it was creepy.

"You said off and on, Evan. Where else was she staying?"

Evan shifted in his seat. His gaze danced around. "My

sisters' places. Mostly Penny."

"I'm sorry about Penny."

"Yeah, me, too." Evan took a long drag of his cigarette. "Penny was the oldest. Our dad died when she was young. Penny was never the same, my ma says. She became like a parent to Claire. Her death, Claire missing, it's too much." He held up his cigarette. "I can't afford to drink no more. My PO—that's my probation officer—says it will be a slippery slope to the slammer. I'm getting my life back now. Don't need another complication."

"I can understand."

"*Can you?*" Nearly shouting. His sudden mood swing caught Megan off guard. "You prance in here smelling good and looking like you ain't missed a meal in ten years. Know what Claire had to do to make ends meet? Hustle. She hustled men until she met Martin. It was Martin who settled her down." He pointed his cigarette at Megan. "You can't understand what it was like. Living off some measly monthly amount. Watching your ma work two, three jobs. Having an older sister give up her dreams to take care of us." He glanced at his own hand, seem to regard it as though it was something alien and apart. "Watch your own world fall apart."

"No, I can't know. You're right. And I'm sorry to have barged in here, Evan. I shouldn't have come."

Only by now, Evan had calmed down. He gave her an apologetic smile. "Now you see why I used to drink. Anger management issues—that's what my PO says." He waved at Megan. "You're fine, you're fine. I miss my sisters, that's all. It's nice to have some company."

"I want to help find Claire."

He regarded her with an even look. "I believe you do." Evan stubbed out his cigarette into a glass Mason jar filled halfway with water and lit another. "When Claire was little, she used to want to act. Ma had an old sewing machine. Claire taught herself to sew. She made costumes and dresses, even shirts for me. She had a creative streak. Would put on little plays, show off."

A thing for acting that morphed into conning as an adult? It was possible. "What can you tell me about her relationship with David von Tressler?"

Megan braced herself for another outburst. Instead, Evan sat back against the recliner and looked thoughtful.

"David was a mixed bag. In some ways, he was good for Claire. I think she genuinely loved him. Or thought she did."

"Did he love her?"

Evan seemed surprised by the question. "Did he love Claire? Well, he lost his position at the company for her, so maybe." He took two puffs of his cigarette and blew the smoke out in concentric circles, watching them fade into the air. "Yes, I think David loved my sister. His own wife—have you met her, she's his second—is a real witch. She always has to have her way. Tried to bully Claire. Even had her mother calling my sister."

Megan's impression after meeting Veronica was that she was likely the one whom Claire was really afraid of. Evan seemed to be supporting that conclusion.

"How did they bully your sister?"

"Threats, mostly."

"Did Claire's affair with David continue after they were found out?"

"I don't know. Does it really matter?"

"She's missing. Your sister Penny has been murdered. Don't you think it all matters?"

The anger started to flare in Evan's eyes again. This time, though, he sucked on his cigarette until it was a slow simmer. "I don't know. She comes and goes as she pleases. Sometimes she stays here, sometimes she doesn't. I don't ask questions. That's probably why she likes staying with me best of all." He waved a hand. "But I ain't seen her since any of this started."

"Before Penny...before things happened, did you hear from Penny or Olive while they were in Winsome?"

Evan nodded. "Penny called me all excited. She met a famous mystery author. She thought I would think that was cool." Evan smiled. "She was always worrying about me, trying to make me feel better about myself. I think she even told this woman about me."

"Pretty cool."

"Oh, yeah."

"Did your sister ever mention me? Megan Sawyer?"

Evan shook his head. "Nah. I would have remembered. Why?"

Megan decided to be honest. "She seemed to be researching me before she died. But no one knows why. Any ideas?"

Evan spent a minute lighting up another cigarette before responding. He seemed to be thinking about the question.

"Penny was always into something. I know she was working on some project, but I have no idea what it was."

"Do you know anyone who might know? A husband? Kids? From the little I could tell about your sister, she lived alone."

"Penny divorced years ago. Husband was a nice enough guy, but no ambition, works a few miles from here, at the wine store. Doubt he'd know much, but you could ask. They stayed friendly." He shrugged shrunken shoulders. "No kids, though. Claire would be a better bet. She told Claire a lot of things. But I guess you can't ask Claire." He shook his head. Rubbed watery eyes. "I just want Claire to be okay."

"You and Claire are close," Megan said softly.

"Not really. But we're family. In this crazy world, that's gotta be worth something."

Nineteen

The Wine Library was a sommelier's dream. Situated on a busy corner of Route 202 in Flemington, the mega-store provided a tour around the globe through its bottled offerings. Megan started with the front help desk and asked a petite silver-haired woman for Mr. Greenleaf.

"Spain," she said without looking up. "Or Argentina."

The aisle that housed the Spanish wines was empty, so Megan found her way to Argentina. A plump twenty-something in a plaid mini skirt was bending over the Malbecs; otherwise, that aisle was empty, too. Megan moved on to Chile. There she spotted a sixty-ish man wearing The Wine Library's requisite maroon uniform. He seemed focused on hanging a sign over a row of wines, so she approached him slowly.

"Mr. Greenleaf?"

It took the man a moment to acknowledge her. When he did, his gaze went from blank to wary in seconds. Once likely a blonde, he now had a full head of white hair and a yellowing beard that hid pock-marked skin. Sloping shoulders gave way to wiry arms and a round mid-section. He was a few inches taller than Megan, but he had a way of slouching that made him seem shorter.

"I need this job," he hissed. "Please. Not sure who sent you, but I don't do that here."

Megan shook her head. "I'm just here to talk to you about your ex-wife, Penny. My name is Megan Sawyer."

"You're not looking for...no, well, that's good...anyway, I'm working. I can't afford to lose this job...you know. Penny, huh? Poor Penny." He spoke in a meandering monotone that made him hard to follow.

"I just need a few minutes of your time."

"You with the police? I already told them what I know, which is nothing."

"No, I'm not. Penny's body was found on my farm. I'm anxious to find who did it."

Greenleaf smoothed his mustache with a nicotine-stained pointer finger. "What I said before, about my job? I really can't lose it...bills, liens...you get it."

"Of course." The twenty-something moved into the Chile aisle carrying a bottle of white wine. Megan glanced at her and said, "Any chance you can take a break, Mr. Greenleaf? Happy to buy you a soda or something."

"Barry. Call me Barry." He rubbed at his mustache again, absentmindedly, while he watched the twenty-something woman. "I could sure use a cigarette. Smoker...you know...can't quit. We could go out back for five. I'm due that. Just give me...I need a few minutes to finish."

Megan waited for Barry at the end of the aisle. When he was finished, he went behind the help desk, murmured something to the woman behind the counter, and nodded at whatever she said in reply. The woman gave Megan the once over before returning to a computer kiosk.

"Got five, that's it." Barry walked ahead of Megan to the far exit. "Have to smoke out here. You know how it is." Outside, at the end of the parking lot, he said, "Want one?" He held out the packet.

Megan shook her head. "Thanks, but I don't smoke."

Barry leaned against a cement pole. He took a cigarette out of the packet and lit it. "So Penny was found at your place. Police question you?"

"Of course."

Eyes narrowed. "You under suspicion and now you're trying to find someone else to pin it on?"

"That's not it at all. I live with my grandmother. We don't feel safe. I want this nightmare to be over."

Barry tilted his head while he took another puff. His eyes were bloodshot, and in the harsh glare of the sunlight, Megan noticed that what wasn't red was a jaundiced yellow. Liver disease? Maybe healthcare was the reason Barry Greenleaf needed his job so badly.

Barry huffed out a sigh and said, "Penny and I were married forever ago. We stayed friends, but we weren't close. No kids. Not even a dog to share." He laughed, a faraway look in his eyes. "She had a wicked sense of humor and a mean sense of justice." He dropped the cigarette and stomped on it. "We met at a rally in New York City. Put an end to chlorofluorocarbons, or something like that. CFCs...they burn a hole in the ozone layer. You know about CFCs? Not cool."

Megan nodded. She knew about CFCs. "Not cool at all. So you met at a protest, and then you got married?"

"Married two years, divorced thirty."

"That's a long time to stay friends."

Barry smiled. "Penny and I had chemistry, but we quickly found that's where it ended. I thought I wanted a family, she definitely didn't. She was devoted to her music, I wasn't devoted to anything." Another faraway smile. "We parted amicably, as they say. Few years ago, I lost my job at the pharmaceutical company up the road. Maintenance. Have some health issues, needed insurance. Penny hooked me up with this place."

"That was nice."

"That was Penny. She cared about people."

"She never remarried?"

"Nah. She was more interested in ideals and missions that marriage." Barry pulled out another cigarette, stared at it longingly, then put it back. "Supposed to quit. Doc says it's killing me." He rubbed at his mustache. "I'm sorry, but I need to get back in there."

"I understand. I appreciate your time. Anything else you can think of before you go? Something she was working on? A project?"

Barry sighed. "Penny was always working on something. Last we spoke, she said something about tying up loose ends."

Loose ends? That sounded ominous. "Any idea what she meant by that?"

"No idea whatsoever. I asked her, and she told me to mind my business." He chuckled. "She was always telling me to mind my business and focus on my health. Would have made a good mother. Always mothering someone."

"Mr. Greenleaf...Barry, did you know that Penny's sister, Claire, is missing?"

Barry's eyes widened and his mouth went slack. "I didn't know." He shook his head. "The cops asked me if I'd seen her. They never told me she was missing. Is it possible...could she be...maybe the same killer who got Penny got her?"

"Now you understand my worry."

Barry tucked the pack of cigarettes in his pants pocket. Sloped shoulders even more slumped, he looked up at the sky. "CFCs, murder, now this. The world is not a just place."

"No, it isn't always just," Megan said.

He turned to go without another word. She watched as

Barry Greenleaf went back into The Wine Library, her mind on protests and chlorofluorocarbons and one woman's "loose ends."

It was after three when Megan finally returned to Winsome. The heat and humidity of the morning had reached a crescendo, with violent thunderstorms that made her return nerve-racking and slow. She had stopped by the café to check on Bibi and Bibi's car, and, satisfied that both were fine, went back to the farm. Thankfully, the rain had stopped, although the sudden torrent left the fields and walkways muddy.

She found Porter in the barn, washing kale and arugula for Alvaro. "The king needs ten pounds of kale and three of arugula," Porter said, making a face. "Who wants ten pounds of kale?"

Megan smiled. "Alvaro."

"Said he's making some twist on spanakopita for tomorrow's dinner special. Should be interesting."

"Always is. Have you heard from Clay?" Megan asked.

"It's his day off, so I wouldn't expect to. Have heard from Ryan, though. He asked for you to pop up to the Marshall house when you have time."

Curious, Megan made her way there. The field between the two properties was rain-soaked and fragrant with the scents of wildflowers. Megan stepped carefully, avoiding nettles and heavy grasses. She reminded herself to have Clay and Porter put a path in between the properties—a real stone path, so no one needed to get muddy or tick-covered when traveling between the houses.

Ryan was outside putting down sod. He waved when he saw Megan.

"Figured the rain was over for a spell. Look nice?"

It did, and Megan said so. "Everything looks great. How's the septic coming?"

"We should have that fixed up in another few days. Then the house will be pretty much ready to go." He smiled. "Want to see inside? The caretaker apartment is finished."

Megan followed Ryan through the front door.

"Sorry about the heat. Central air should be installed later this week."

Megan fanned herself with a piece of paper she found on a stool. "Once that happens, I'll have to come up here to cool down."

Ryan nodded. "We've modernized everything. Put in new ducking so that the whole house will have air." He led her through the kitchen, which was white and shiny and perfect for commercial cooking, and to a locked door.

"Voila." He fiddled with the lock and held the door open for Megan.

She stepped through the threshold and took in a sharp breath. It was amazing to see their plans come to life. A small slate-floored foyer with a closet and bench opened up to a large living room, dining room, kitchen combination. Hardwood floors, vaulted ceilings, white Shaker kitchen cabinets, and picture windows made the open space feel cozy and modern. A fireplace with flanking bookshelves matched the Colonial style of the house.

"Come through here," Ryan said.

He led Megan into a modest bedroom with a walk-in closet and small en-suite bathroom with a large shower stall. "On the other side is another small closet and a half bath."

"It's perfect."

Ryan pointed to a control panel on the wall. "Zoned heating

and cooling for this apartment. If you have guests, you can maintain separate temperature zones."

"What can I say? I love it."

Ryan grinned. "I hoped you would. I put in extra insulation for sound proofing for dogs or kids or whatever, and made sure there was plenty of storage."

"You've thought of everything."

"I try."

As they walked back into the home's center hall, Megan said, "To think, we almost didn't get to work together. I was scheduled to use Duke Masterman. Do you know him?"

Ryan's eyes narrowed, he frowned. "Duke? Yeah, we all know him. Gives contractors a bad name."

"Then you know he's bailed on some work."

"Oh, I know it all right. I've been cleaning up his messes across Winsome. Guy just stopped showing up." Ryan shook his head. "Look, this line of business is rough. It's often feast or famine, but that's no excuse. You take money, you finish a job." He frowned again. "Did he screw you out of funds?"

"No, he returned our deposit. But he cost us precious time. Do you think he's okay? I haven't even seen him around town."

Ryan locked the door leading into the caretaker's apartment and put his key ring back into his pocket. "Who knows what he's up to. He's young and single. Never really liked him. Unreliable." He glanced at Megan. "Sounds like you got a taste of that."

"Sure did."

"Consider yourself lucky. If he left you that easily, he'd do it to the next person as well."

He already has, Megan thought. *Good riddance.*

Twenty

Megan spent the rest of the afternoon thinking about Duke Masterman. Young and single, Ryan had said—and he was right. Young and single and handsome. Megan had known Duke since they were kids in high school, which is why she figured she would employ him for the Marshall house renovations. Broad shouldered and muscular, with a shaved head and a "Mother" tattoo on his left bicep, Duke carried himself with the confidence of a hardcore gym rat. But he'd always been friendly, and the reviews of his work were strong. Duke lost both his parents when he was in his early thirties, and he'd inherited their house on the far end of Canal Street—an old, small Tudor cottage that Duke had lovingly restored.

Once the weeds were pulled and the microgreens seeds planted, Megan decided to swing by the Masterman house to see for herself if he was home. She loaded some extra tatsoi and cherry tomatoes into the truck for Alvaro, and headed out.

It was early evening, and Winsome seemed quiet after the long weekend's festivities. Remnants of yesterday's celebration—bits of streamers, a stray tent here and there—littered the downtown area. Remmy Booker still had tables set outside her yarn shop from the sidewalk sale, and the tent where the salsa band had played was only half deconstructed. But overall, the town looked pretty and quaint and solid, a town that had withstood hundreds of years, and would withstand many more to come.

If "development" didn't irrevocably alter it.

Already the signs were there. The Walmart a mile outside of town. The independent bookstore off Canal Street that closed last year, unable to compete with the big box stores or online retailers. The small enclave of million-dollar houses on quarter acre lots that went up on part of an old farm property. And, of course, the von Tressler mansion: a house now situated on a wooded hill that had remained wooded since the Revolutionary War.

That was the nature of life, Megan knew, but the knowing didn't change the ache much. What would Winsome look like in a hundred years? A decade? Would it simply be part of a characterless extension of the Philadelphia suburbs?

Megan pulled up to the café. She idled there for a moment, looking into the store she and Bibi and the Hands had built, feeling nostalgic. Even on a Tuesday at six o'clock, it was bustling. Alvaro had challenged the norm with ethnic-inspired farm-to-table food, and his fare brought in people from all over. Megan sold nothing touched by glyphosate, and sales were the best they'd ever been. People paid twice as much for local handmade soaps and lotions and scarves than what they would have for cheap products made in mass quantities overseas and sold at large chain stores.

Maybe there was hope.

Her mind flitted to her conversation with Denver at the fish and chip place in Philly. Change wasn't always bad. Taking a risk could pay back tenfold. She was scared, true, but was that a valid reason not to choose a path, especially a path shared with someone she loved. Starting the farm had taken courage. Opening the café had taken courage. True, losing Mick had been the biggest blow of her life, but if she didn't give life with Denver a chance, wasn't she letting fear win?

Megan pulled away from the curb. The Masterman house was another mile down the road. She passed a trio of craftsman-style cottages and then came to Duke's house. The lights were off, the driveway empty. The house sat right on the street with only a strip of flower bed separating it from the road. The flowers looked weedy and in need of care.

Megan climbed out of the truck. She started with the front door, knocking loudly. No answer. She rang the bell. Nothing. Duke had put a privacy fence around the small backyard, but the gate had no lock. Megan let herself in. The grass in the rear of the property was overgrown. Other than that, the yard was neat, the small brick patio tidy.

A peek inside a ground floor window exposed a clean kitchen. No sign of Duke.

You're a regular Peeping Tina, Megan thought to herself. She was waiting for a neighbor to call the police. She decided to head that off. Back in the front yard, Megan looked over at the triplet craftsman cottages. The one closest to Duke's had a car parked out front. Megan knocked on the door.

An older woman Megan didn't know glanced out from behind a chain locked door.

"Yes?"

"I'm looking for Duke Masterman, your neighbor, ma'am," Megan said. "It doesn't appear he's been home for a while. Have you seen him?"

"You with the police?"

"No, I'm not." Megan introduced herself. "I knew Duke from school. Just checking up on him."

"The police been by, too. Wonder what Duke's gotten himself messed up in." The woman unlocked the door and came out onto her small porch. "You Bonnie Birch's granddaughter?"

"I sure am."

"I thought so. I've seen your photo in the town paper." A warm smile lit up her face. "Gertrude Ellsworth. Bonnie calls me Gertie. We play Bridge together."

Megan had heard Bibi talk about Gertie on occasion. "Happy to meet you."

"Where are my manners? Would you like to come in? I just finished supper and I have some nice minestrone soup left over. I can fix you a bowl."

"No, thank you, Gertie. I need to get to the store. I was just hoping maybe you've seen Duke."

"It's Duke you're after, huh? I thought Bibi said you were practically engaged to that handsome Dr. Finn. He's a catch, that one." She smiled again. "But then, you are, too. You treat Bonnie well. She tells us all the time how you dote on her. We all wish we had a grandchild like you. Not sure why she'd even be looking at Serenity Manor. If I were your grandmother, I'd stay right where I was."

"Serenity Manor?"

"She took a tour with us last week. I'm interested in living there, and I mentioned it in passing. I told her it was silly for her to go. She insisted."

Megan was sure the shock was apparent on her face. A retirement home? Somedays she felt like having her and her dogs in the house was a lot for Bibi, but she'd never indicated a desire to leave. Bibi loved the farm. She was active and engaged, and being useful was something Bibi cherished. But the painkillers...was there something her grandmother wasn't telling her?

"Duke, Megan?" Gertie said, reminding Megan why she was here.

"I'm not here for Duke in that way. He had done some work for someone I know, and they said he hasn't shown up in a few weeks. I wanted to make sure he's okay."

"The police are concerned, too." She glanced over at Duke's house, running a hand through her white wedge cut in the process. "Last time I saw Duke was maybe two, three weeks ago. He's a skirt chaser, if you know what I mean. I wouldn't normally say that, but you being Bonnie's granddaughter and all. I kind of figured he had found some woman and was staying there."

"Have you known him to do that before?"

"He's always come and gone as he pleased, especially since his father passed." She crossed herself. "Used to fight with his parents something awful. Nice enough man, but temperamental. Have to watch what you say to him."

Megan knew what she meant. In the short time they'd worked together, he had been adamant about having control of the project and his crew. Didn't like to be questioned. Megan felt again like she'd dodged a cannon.

"Thanks, Gertie. I appreciate the information. Out of curiosity, was it Bobby King who talked to you about Duke?"

"No, some woman I didn't know. Little thing. Cute, with brown hair. Cheekbones to die for."

Megan's pulse increased a few beats. "Thanks again. Have fun at Bridge."

"Tell Bonnie to stop beating me. You'd think that woman would get tired of winning."

Megan laughed. "Bibi? Never. She lives for the kill."

Parked in front of the café, Megan called King from the truck. He didn't answer, so she left him a message. She decided to try

Dominick von Tressler as well on the off chance he was working late. No receptionist this time, just a voicemail system. She left him a cryptic message, and asked him to call her back.

As she was getting out of the truck, her cell phone rang. It was Bobby.

"I'm glad you called, Megan. I need to talk with you. Will you be home later?"

"I'm at the café now, then I'm planning to meet Denver for a late dinner at the tavern. Want to join us? Eight o'clock."

King hesitated, but only for a second. "Sounds good. I'll see you then."

Inside the café, Megan found her grandmother at the counter eating a plate of leftover cauliflower tacos from the Fourth of July dinner.

"Pretty good," she said while stabbing a fork full of avocado salad. "My mother used to have to force me to eat cauliflower. Who knew you could dress it up like this?" She patted the empty seat next to her. "Come sit. Have some tacos."

"I have dinner with Denver later. You're welcome to join us."

Bibi shook her head. "My favorite shows are on tonight. Alvaro promised me some sopapillas with honey. After that, it's home for me."

The restaurant had emptied out, and only two families were still eating in the café. Clover was at the register chatting with Clay, who had a pile of groceries in front of him. Megan excused herself and joined the Hands.

"You were looking for me?" she said to Clay. "I've tried calling you back."

"I didn't think it was urgent. We can catch up tomorrow," Clay said. He looked tired. Megan noticed paint on his knuckles and what looked like dried putty on the hairs of his arm.

"Spending your day off working on your apartment?"

"Not exactly." He paid his sister for the groceries and loaded them into his knapsack.

Megan was stung by his curt tone. "You okay?"

"I wish you would have mentioned that you were lending me out."

"What are you talking about?"

"Me, working for someone else. You agreeing to it."

Megan had no idea what he was talking about—at first. Then it dawned on her. "Ah, Melanie."

"She approached me in town yesterday morning. Said you said I'd be happy to make some extra cash at her place." He held up his left hand. "Spent the day spackling and painting a master bedroom that's the size of my whole apartment." He threw the knapsack over his shoulder. "If you'll excuse me, I need to get some sleep. We have the big Philly restaurant order we have to deliver tomorrow. I'll be over early—around five."

"I can do that, Clay. Porter and I will wash everything up, bag it, and I can drive it into the city. Sleep in."

Clay's expression softened. "That's okay. It's not like I didn't get paid for today. I just wish you'd warned me." Clay started to walk away, and Megan placed a hand on his shoulder.

"Hear me out. *Please.*" Clay stopped, turned. "I didn't mention it because I told her no, that I wasn't okay with her asking you. I also said it was ultimately up to you, so I suppose I should have told you about the conversation, but I never thought she'd approach you. And I really never thought she'd lie." Megan held his gaze. "I didn't loan you or Porter out. I would never do that."

Clay nodded. He glanced at Clover, then back at Megan. "She really made it sound like it was a deal between friends. I'm sorry for accusing you."

"It's okay. I have a feeling Melanie doesn't accept 'no' lightly."

"For sure." Clay shifted his weight, adjusting the bag on his back. "Her mother was there, too. Veronica. She said Melanie is terrified and wants to get the house ready for sale."

"Scared? Of what?" Clover asked.

"She believes she's next on a hit list. Wants to leave Winsome, and she's in a rush to get out from under the house." He shrugged. "I assume she thinks Penny's murderer is after her as well."

"Melanie mentioned to me that she's scared, but she also told me she's staying in Winsome," Megan said. "She blatantly told me her mother twists the truth."

"Also known as a lie," Bibi said, joining them. "I overheard part of your conversation. I don't think it's the first time the von Tresslers have twisted the truth to get what they wanted."

"What do you mean, Bonnie?" Clay asked.

"Roger was in here earlier. When the family applied for the permit to build that house, David said they would place the surrounding woods into conservation. Also said their company would make some investments in Winsome, support the Beautification Board. They haven't done either, and when Roger mentioned it to Melanie, she acted as though she had no idea what he was talking about."

"Sounds like them," Clover said.

"The master bedroom, Clay, was anyone staying in it?" Megan asked.

Clay shook his head. "Still empty. Melanie said she and David had been staying in one of the six guest rooms." He scowled. "A real hardship."

"Don't judge," Clover said, but her reprimand sounded half-hearted. "Why do you ask, Megan?"

"Just curious. Did you happen to see the room she's staying in?" Megan asked Clay.

"The master is in a separate hall, so no. Why?"

"Just wondering."

"Whether she shared it with David?" Bibi asked. "I was wondering the very same thing."

Twenty-One

"Three ales, one order of Bavarian pretzels, a brisket sandwich," Denver said, "and whatever these two are having." He glanced over at King. "Dinner's my treat, so eat up."

"Cobb salad, hold the ham," Megan said. "And an iced tea to balance out the ale."

"Burger and fries." King perused the menu. "And since Denver's paying, add in a Caesar side salad."

The waitress walked away, and King leaned in. "Shall I go first, Megan."

"Right to business," Denver said.

"It's this bloody von Tressler-Greenleaf mess. I'm getting political pressure to clean things up, and we have zero leads. Zip. Megan was our most obvious lead, and we know where that went." He clapped his beefy hands. "A few more questions, friendly this time."

Megan felt Denver bristle beside her. She put a calming hand on his forearm. "Shoot."

"The coroner puts the time of death for Penelope between nine and noon on Thursday. I told you that. Based on the position of the body, the test results, etc., she thinks the body was moved immediately to its resting place on your property."

"Okay? You told me that as well." Megan didn't know where he was going with this line of questioning. This was nothing new.

"Where was Ryan and his crew? If a body had been moved to the Marshall property in broad daylight, wouldn't they have seen it happen?"

Megan thought about that. She tried to remember what was happening Thursday morning. She had been at the café. Merry had swung by. King, too. But she hadn't talked with Ryan—she'd just assumed he was at the house. Later, when she and Bibi were touring the barn, it had been Ryan's crew who found the body, so they had arrived at some point.

"You don't seriously suspect Ryan?" she said. This time it was Denver who placed a calming hand on her arm. "Now you're grasping at anything."

King shook his head. "We have no reason to suspect Ryan Craig of anything. But it does seem odd, doesn't it? I have a call in to your contractor to see what was happening that day, but if the coroner is right, and I have no reason to doubt her, why didn't they see the perpetrator at the house?"

"I don't know. I'll ask Ryan. And if you get him first, let me know."

"Is that it?" Denver said.

The waitress came by with three ales and a heaping plate of their homemade soft pretzels. "The pretzels are on the house. Our thanks to the Chief."

"Awe, Kelly, Denver here is paying this time."

The waitress flashed a gorgeous smile. "I'll get you next time, too."

King's smiled lingered as the waitress walked away.

"Watch it, or Megan will tell Clover," Denver said. He picked up his ale and took a drink.

"Clover has nothing to worry about. Just because you've already ordered doesn't mean you can't look at the menu."

"I think it does," Denver said.

Megan laughed. "What else, King? Surely you have more than Ryan's missing hours."

King had attacked the pretzels. He was in the middle of dipping a wedge into a bowl of the tavern's signature beer-cheese sauce when he said, "We've been looking at Penny's laptop files, trying to figure out the connection to you."

Megan's pulse quickened. This was what she had been hoping to hear. "And?"

"Does that name 'Edwin Tyler' ring any bells?"

"No. Should it?"

"How about Ned Buttons?"

"No, sorry."

"Mack McGready? Mitchell Barski? Len Salvo?"

"No, no, and no. Why?"

King sighed and reached for another pretzel. "These were names in the file she kept about you. We're looking into them, but I was hoping you'd know who they were."

Megan shook her head slowly back and forth. "Can you give me the names again? I want to write them down." Megan jotted them as King repeated each one. "Got it, thanks."

"Let me know if you figure it out."

"I will. Are you still thinking the file Penny kept on me is somehow connected to the motive for Penny's murder?"

"I don't know, but as someone wise taught me, there are generally no such things as coincidences."

Megan smiled. "My Aunt Sarah was by, Bobby. She told me Penny reached out to her as well. She said Penny seemed nice enough, but she was asking weird questions about me a few days before she was killed."

"She called the station and reported it," King said. "Didn't really add anything new."

Megan looked at King over the rim of her ale. "She said Penny loved mysteries, was a big fan." Megan thought about what Evan had said about his big sister. "The impression I've gotten of Penny is a woman who cared deeply for her family, often putting them before herself."

King nodded. "That's the impression I get, too. But there can be a fine line between concern and control. Which is why Claire's disappearance and Penny's death worry me."

"I don't follow," Denver said.

"Megan, you and Merry both described a very distraught Claire the day of the memorial," King said. "Both Olive and Penny were trying to calm her down, but Claire remained upset. Crying, wailing. Olive has told me that she pushed Claire to stand up for herself. To fight for her portion of the von Tressler fortune."

"She told me that, too," Megan said.

"Both Melanie and Claire's brother, Evan James, told me that Claire really loved David."

"Same," Megan said.

"Still not following, Bobby," Denver said.

King drained his stein and pushed it away. He signaled to the waitress for another. "What if Claire had been fixated on David. What if her love turned to obsession?"

"And Penny, realizing her sister had gone over the edge, had stepped in to stop her." Megan saw what King was suggesting, and it made sense. "That may even have been the reason Claire disappeared. She needed to get away."

King wagged a pretzel at Megan. "Right. Claire overreacts and kills her sister."

"The flowers Claire bought were in the makeshift grave with Penny," Megan said, picturing the lavish bouquet, dry, sullied, and lifeless. "They may have seen each other sometime between the dinner they crashed with me and Denver and the next morning, when Penny was set to return home."

King nodded. "If Claire was the one, she may also be the one who threw the rock into Melanie's window. Her obsession with David could still be alive and well, and now she's taking aim at Melanie."

Megan thought about that. It would explain a lot. Her despair at David's death, Melanie's worry about her own safety, and Claire's continued disappearance.

"What about the slashed tires? Did you get an answer on whether the sisters' car tire had been slashed?" Megan asked.

"Not yet," King said.

"How do you explain Duke Masterman's sudden disappearance? Is that connected?" Megan asked. She told him about her visit to Duke's house. "His neighbor, Gertrude, hasn't seen him in weeks. She thought he was shacked up with some woman, as she put it."

"Yeah, kind of figured as much. Duke's never been known for discretion."

Megan said, "So you did talk to Gertrude."

"The neighbor?"

"Yes. She said the police talked with her."

King looked confused. "No one has filed a missing person on Masterman. Just because he left town without telling anyone doesn't make him missing, so we'd have no reason to track his whereabouts. We have enough on our plates."

"What about the fact that he walked away from the von Tressler job without finishing, effectively stealing the rest of their money?" Megan asked.

"Neither Melanie nor David filed charges. Not my problem, and right now, I have enough problems." King glanced at Megan. "What's wrong? You look like you've seen a ghost."

"I think I may have." Megan swallowed, hard. "Gertrude said the police questioned her. A young detective. Tiny, brunette. Great cheekbones. Any chance she was one of yours?"

King's eyes narrowed to slits. "No, but maybe something happened I wasn't aware of. Been kind of busy." He dialed a number on his cell and had a brief conversation with dispatch. "Waiting for a call back," he said. A few seconds later, the phone rang. King listened, thanked the caller, and hung up.

"Well?" Denver said.

"No missing person report, no police inquiry. That wasn't our detective."

"Small. Brunette. Young." Megan repeated.

"Like Claire von Tressler," King said, eyes slowly widening.

"A ghost indeed," Denver said. "And Megs, you and I both know where ghosts reside."

Twenty-Two

True to his word, Clay was at the farm and working by five the next morning. Megan had climbed out of bed reluctantly at four thirty, checked on Bibi, who was still sleeping soundly, and tiptoed downstairs with Sadie and Gunther to make coffee and some granola. She found Porter's dog in the kitchen, snoring softly by the back door, and gave Sarge a rub behind the ears.

Once everyone was fed, she and the dogs met Clay and Porter at the barn. They had orders from three prominent Philadelphia restaurants to fill, and butter lettuce, Romaine, scallions, and arugula had to be carefully washed and packaged. One stray grasshopper, one ladybug, and even their organic practices wouldn't save them. No one wanted a bug in their salad.

Clay washed and Megan and Porter inspected and packaged. They worked quietly while Gunther and Sarge slept outside in the shade. Sadie had disappeared inside with the goats where it was cool.

It was nearly eight when they placed the last of the packages in separately marked coolers. "Load them in the truck," Megan said, "and I'll be off."

"I told you I'd do it," Clay said. "I really am sorry about yesterday. Accusing you and all."

"I'm not upset, Clay. The truth is, I have an ulterior motive for heading into the city."

"Let me at least go with you."

Megan refused. "You and Porter can start getting ready for the farmers market. Figure out how much we can bring, what will be ready to harvest. Plus, the rear bed is in desperate need of weeding, and the compost needs some attention."

Clay didn't argue. He helped to load the coolers in the truck before heading out to the back beds. Megan figured he'd do the most labor-intensive work while the morning was still relatively cool. She ran to the house to change into something more professional.

When she came back out, Porter was standing by the truck. "You look awful dressed up to deliver lettuce."

"I have something I need to attend to while I'm in the city."

Porter frowned. "I wish you'd let all of this go. Let King handle it."

Megan searched Porter's eyes. "Why? What has you worried?"

Brian looked out at the fields. His gaze landed on Sarge and he whistled for the dog.

"Brian?" Megan said again.

"I thought I heard something last night. I left the barn to investigate, and by the time I got outside the noises had stopped."

"What kind of noises?"

"Thumping. I don't know, could have been a woodpecker or an owl or a branch hitting a window."

Only there are no branches near the windows, Megan thought. "But you think someone was out there."

"I do." Porter hung his head. "You and Bibi and Denver and Clay...I don't have family. You're it. Let King handle this."

Megan lifted Porter's chin with two fingers. "We love you,

too."

Porter laughed, eyes downcast. "Megan."

"Look, I promise to be careful, okay?"

Porter's lips pressed together. "Okay."

Megan was about to drive away when something occurred to her. "Brian, you and Duke Masterman, you hung out with some of the same people."

"In my party days, yeah. Why?"

"He the kind of guy who would up and disappear for weeks on end?"

Porter snorted. "Yeah, definitely. I liked to party, Duke *loves* to party."

"Anyone in his life tying him down? Family, a girlfriend?"

Porter's eyes narrowed, his forehead creased in concentration. "Hmmm...back then, no. Now, who knows."

"Any reason you can think of why he'd dump his current projects and run?"

"Absolutely. Dude's a hard worker, I'll give him that, but he's always working to feed the beast."

The beast? "Drugs and alcohol?"

"Nah. Lady Chance." Porter slapped the hood of Megan's truck. "Blackjack, roulette, slots, races, you name it. Duke is a gambling addict. At least he was back then."

On her way into the city, Megan called Roger's house. His wife Anita answered.

"Megan, I'm so happy to hear from you. How are you and that wonderful grandmother of yours?"

"We're well, Anita. Any chance Jenny is home?" Megan explained that she wanted to talk to Roger's niece.

"No, I'm sorry. She picked up a job at a local retirement

community, Serenity Manor over in Chalfont. She'll be there until tonight."

"Do you know if she gets a break?"

"I don't, but you can ask her. I'll give you her phone number."

Megan pulled the truck over and copied the digits. After thanking Anita, she texted Jenny a request to meet with her later that day.

Back on the road, she ran through things she wanted to do. Drop off the vegetables. Talk to Dominick. And check on the von Tressler property one more time.

We know where ghosts reside, Denver had said. Megan suspected the light she'd seen was no apparition. Claire may very well have found her way home.

It was after eleven that morning when Megan finally dropped off the last produce order. She checked her phone before heading toward Center City and von Tressler Investments. Jenny had gotten back to her. She was booked up today, but she suggested coffee at the retirement community mid-morning tomorrow. She had a break then and could spend some time chatting.

Megan accepted.

Parking downtown was hard to come by, so Megan paid for an hour in a guarded lot and walked the two blocks to Arch Street. Von Tressler Investments was located in a high-rise building. Two guards greeted Megan in the lobby.

"I'm here to see Dominick von Tressler," Megan told the older of the guards. She removed her driver's license from her wallet and slid it across the counter. "Here you go."

"Is he expecting you?"

"Yes." Megan figured that wasn't a total lie. She had told

him she'd stop by in person in her voicemail message.

The guard studied her license without a trace of emotion. He dialed an extension and then announced Megan's presence to whomever answered. "I'm sorry," the guard said, not sounding a bit sorry, "The receptionist says you're not on Mr. von Tressler's calendar."

"Can you call him directly."

"I'm sorry. You need an appointment, or Mr. von Tressler has to give permission to let you up."

"Right, so please call him."

"I'm sorry. You don't have an appointment." He slid her license back across the counter.

It's like a damn Kafka novel, Megan thought. Behind Megan, people in business suits and business casual twin sets came in and out of the building, and a line was forming behind her. The elevator banks were behind the guards. Megan considered running for the elevators but decided against it. She'd call Dominick again. Or maybe she would wait outside the building, like a stalker. She headed back to her truck.

The ride from Center City to Chestnut Hill took longer than Megan anticipated. Route 76 was backed up, so Megan took Kelly Drive. It wasn't much better. A curvy twenty-minute drive took nearly forty. The von Tressler street was blissfully devoid of traffic, and Megan climbed out of the truck, grateful for the sudden calm.

The house looked different in daylight. So ominous-looking at night, now it seemed stately and handsome and majorly in need of repair. The bushes and flower beds were overgrown, sure, but under the glare of the midday sun, they appeared unkempt and forlorn, not malevolent.

Megan knocked on the door, rang the bell, and waited. No response.

She stepped back to look up at the upper floors when she heard the sound of a truck behind her. She turned to see a landscape crew arrive at the house. One man pulled a mower off the trailer while another revved up a weedwhacker.

"Excuse me," Megan said to the man with the mower, "have you seen the woman who lives here?"

He shook his head. "No women." His accent was heavy and hard to decipher.

"Do you know who is paying for the service?"

The man shrugged.

The other man turned off the weedwhacker and joined them by the entryway. "Is there a problem?"

"No, not at all. I'm trying to locate the woman who lives here."

"No one lives here. Not as long as we've been coming."

"Do you know who is paying for the service?"

The landscaper shook his head. "Whoever it is, they keep paying the bills. Wish they'd pay for us to do the back, too. It sure is a mess. Makes us look like we're unprofessional and do a half-ass job."

He started up the weedwhacker again. Conversation over.

Megan glanced around the street. She spied a Rolls Royce in the driveway of the home next to this one and thought she'd try knocking on the door. This wasn't the kind of neighborhood where someone came knocking, so she doubted the reception would be a welcome one. She was halfway to the neighbor's yard when she felt a tap on her shoulder. She spun around to see the two landscapers standing on the curb behind her, looking mildly curious.

"He says it's a man who owns the house," the weedwhacker said, pointing to the mower.

Megan nodded. "A man used to own it, but he passed

away."

The man with the mower shook his head, his frustration obvious. He said something in a language that sounded eastern European.

"My cousin says it's not Mr. von Tressler."

"Can he describe the man?"

Megan waited while the two men conversed in a foreign tongue.

"Not really. Big muscles. Bald head."

Megan's eyes widened. "A 'Mother' tattoo on his bicep?"

Another quick sidebar conversation, and the landscaper with the weedwhacker said, "Maybe. He just remembers big muscles and a bald head. Shaved, you know. On purpose." The man ran a hand through his own head of thick hair. "He was walking around the property. My cousin said he acted as though he owned it."

Megan thanked the men. They stood there expectantly, and she handed each a ten-dollar bill. As she buckled back into her truck, she thought about what they'd told her. Bald and muscular? Duke Masterman at the von Tressler estate?

Meanwhile, Gertie had described someone who could have been Claire asking about Duke. Were they working together? If so, what were the two of them cooking up?

Megan called King, but he didn't answer. She left him a voicemail asking him to call her back.

As Megan pulled back onto the highway, her phone rang. Assuming it was King, she answered immediately with, "What's up?"

"I received your messages," said an unfamiliar voice. "Dominick von Tressler. The guards told me you came by today."

"Yes, yes. I was hoping we could talk."

"About my uncle?"

"About your uncle and your grandfather."

Silence on the other end. Megan thought he'd hung up, and she was about to do the same, when he said, "Can you be here soon?"

Megan glanced at the truck's dashboard clock. "Thirty minutes?"

"Meet me at Starbucks on Sixteenth Street."

Twenty-Three

Megan recognized Dominick right away. Even in a suit, he looked to her like a teenaged David playing dress-up. He'd found a table in the very rear of the store, next to a woman wearing headphones who was staring at an iPad and nursing a cup of coffee.

Megan shook Dominick's hand and took the seat across from him. "Thanks for seeing me." The Starbucks was crowded, and their voices were drowned out by the chatter of other customers. "I won't take up a lot of your time."

"I've seen you in Winsome," Dominick said, flashing a boyish smile. "And please, call me Dom." He picked up his coffee cup. "Want something?"

"I'm good."

"So what's your interest in my family?"

Megan explained her interaction with Claire, the fact that Penny's body had been planted on her property. She left out the details, painting enough of a picture to—she hoped—justify her nosiness.

"So you're helping the police."

"Not exactly. I feel obligated to do something, all things considered. You seemed like a good person to talk to given your own history with David and Melanie."

"That's one way to put it." He rolled his cup between his

hands. "What is it you want to know about my grandfather and Uncle David? Why they were both such difficult men?" He smiled again to soften his words.

Megan's eyes widened. Right to it, then. "Your grandfather made you head of a very lucrative company. He must have had some redeeming qualities."

Dom laughed—a bitter sound. "Let's see. I was second choice to run the company. Actually, I was probably fifth or sixth choice, but I was family and therefore more manipulable, which made me more desirable. I don't *really* own anything— not in official terms, anyway. And everyone both hates me and kisses my bony arse." He held up his cup in a toast. "Thank you, Grandpa."

"There's a lot to unpack there."

"Not really." Dom placed his cup down and ran a hand over his stubbled chin. He had intelligent eyes, and they bore into Megan's with a startling candor. "My grandfather liked to play games with people. He chased my mother away at a young age with his nonsense. If you understand that about him, then everything makes sense."

"He was playing a game with you?"

"Not me. I was—am—a convenient pawn. He was playing games—still is—with Claire and David."

"I don't follow."

"Because you're probably sane, and the actions of cruel people don't make sense."

Megan waited while he sipped his coffee. He was staring miserably down at his cup, as though it were the reason for all of his problems.

"The truth is very simple. At first I thought my grandfather saw something great in me and I was honored. He paid for my graduate school, mentored me through my career decisions.

After he died...well, his will said it all."

"He left the business to his son, David?"

"No. Nor did he leave it to Claire. Games, remember?"

Megan was starting to feel as though Dom was playing games with her. "Games. I got it."

"In a fit of anger, my grandfather stripped David from his position as head of the company and installed me, with the Board's permission, of course—permission I'm sure he strong-armed from them. When he died, I thought why not? My mother was his daughter. I deserve a break. But it wasn't to be. My grandfather played a game from beyond. He left the business and everything else to the person I choose—but my only choices are Claire or David. I have three years to decide who is more deserving. Three years that are almost up. If I do what he asks, I stay on as CEO and get a 10 percent stake in the business."

Megan said, "But Claire or David are the real owners, and if you pick David, you have someone more qualified looking over your shoulder."

"Older, not more qualified." He pushed his cup across the table, flicked it with his fingers. "Pick Claire, and I have someone who has no idea how to run a business. But my grandfather wasn't finished there. His will mandates documentation submitted to his attorneys about who would be better—and why. And if I fail to make an appropriate choice, bye-bye Dom."

"Who decides what is the appropriate choice?"

Dom shrugged. "See the catch?"

It really was a game—one with no real winner other than Claire or David. She said, "Which is why you were in Winsome."

"Yes. David and Mel were very good at treating me like family. They made it clear who the better choice would be." He sneered. "David."

"And Claire?"

"Claire just wanted David—and the house and the wealth and everything that went with being a Mrs. von Tressler."

"She didn't try to convince you?"

Dom's smile was smug. "She tried a number of things, but her heart wasn't in it. I had decided on David."

Realization dawned on Megan. "And when David died? What did Martin's will say?"

"David's opportunity went to Melanie."

Which would make it a more even playing field for Claire.

As though reading her thoughts, Dom said, "Suddenly a harder decision. Claire had been with Martin for years. Knew his business preferences, acted as his personal assistant. Had a closer connection to Martin. Melanie had been a salesperson for the furniture business. She has more education." He shrugged. "With Claire missing, maybe my decision will be easier."

Megan wasn't so sure. "You've been put in a tough position," Megan said. "Feels like a lose/lose."

Dom nodded. He looked again like a young man—too young for such a burden. "But don't feel too sorry for me. With the experience I've gained, I can go anywhere. Nothing ties me here, especially with my mother, uncle, *and* grandfather gone."

"And if you leave von Tressler investments?"

"*When* I leave, it will be someone else's problem." Reproach colored his cheeks, soured his expression. "Claire's or Melanie's."

Megan tried King again on the way home. No answer. She left another voicemail message, this one more urgent. Martin's will was telling, but so was each party's response. David and Melanie, assuming they were the best candidates, trying to

cajole a "win." Claire doing who knows what to convince him—
and then giving up. Now that David was gone, who would be the
better owner? If Veronica had her way, her daughter would walk
away with the von Tressler fortune, that was clear. If Olive had
her way, Claire would claim what was hers.

Who had more to lose? Melanie was set. If David had left
her the house and whatever assets he had, even without the
company, she could survive. But there was a prenup to consider.
Claire, on the other hand, had been living with a destitute
brother. Losing this battle meant she, perhaps, had nothing.

What an unimaginable mess.

Megan got back to the farm at four. There was a note on the
table from Bibi: *Taking a nap, then having dinner with my
Bridge group. Denver called. Be safe.*

Megan found her grandmother snoozing in the parlor, the
recliner back, another of her afghans across her legs, snoring
softly. The air conditioner had been set to low, and sweat beaded
Bibi's forehead. Megan turned up the air and went upstairs to
change and call Denver.

"Have dinner with me tonight," he said. "I'll cook."

"Annie's squash soup?" Megan asked, harkening back to
their first date.

Denver laughed. The sound warmed her. "I've progressed."

"What time?"

"Six?"

Megan glanced at the clock on her dresser. That would give
her an hour to clean things up here and check on those names
King had given her the day before. "See you then."

"And Megan?"

"Yes?"

"Will you be staying?"

Megan thought of her grandmother asleep on the recliner,

of the painkillers, of Serenity Manor. "I don't think so. Bibi and the steps...I'd be worried, with everything happening...you could come here."

"No one to let the dogs out this evening." A beat went by, and Megan read disappointment into that beat. "It's okay, Megs. As long as you don't have to be home right away, it'll work out."

Six o'clock was approaching fast. Megan had searched all of the names King had given her, and she still didn't come up with any immediate answers. Edwin Tyler seemed to be an operations manager living in Tennessee. Ned Buttons was a retired factory worker from New Jersey. Mack McGready and Len Salvo were deceased. Mitchell Barski, as well as she could tell, was either a schoolteacher in New Hampshire or an industrial safety specialist in Detroit. Either way, she didn't recognize him. She didn't recognize any of them.

At five forty-five, Megan packed up her laptop, grabbed a bottle of wine she had chilling in the refrigerator, bid good-bye to the dogs, and left. A few hours away from this mess was what she needed. A few hours away—and Denver.

Twenty-Four

The first thing Megan noticed were the candles. She opened the door to Denver's house and saw the glow of twenty flames along the fireplace mantel and on the cabinets, above the dogs' reach. The air smelled heavenly—vanilla spice and garlic and roasting meat. Denver had put a champagne flute and a bottle of champagne on the coffee table, and a book by Megan's favorite author next to the champagne.

"In the kitchen, Megs. Put your feet up and relax. Read a book. I'll be in soon."

Smiling, Megan slipped off her sandals and cuddled up on the couch. Denver had five dogs, and his blind beagle and his Golden Retriever joined her. The beagle snuggled against her hip, and Megan leaned over to kiss her sweet head.

"To start." Denver placed a plate of cheese, grapes, and crackers on the table, next to the champagne. He leaned down to kiss her.

"This is lovely. And I love you in that apron."

"Ta." He spun around. He wore a "Winsome is winsome" apron that Bibi had given him. "It suits me." Denver poured two glasses of champagne.

"What are we toasting."

"Life. Us. Dogs. You make the call."

"Us. I like that." She touched the tip of his flute with her own. "What's on the menu?"

Denver pulled Megan up from the couch gently. He tilted her head up and kissed her lips softly. She felt the press of his chest against her, the comfort of his arms around her waist, and she leaned into the kiss.

"That sounds good," she whispered. "I'll have another."

As he peeled off his own shirt, Denver said, "I'll tell you what's *not* on the menu." He kissed her. "Murder." Another kiss. "The von Tressler family." A whispery kiss on her ear. "Bobby King." He unhooked the clasp on Megan's sundress. "Or anything with the word 'police' in it." He pulled her dress over her shoulders, kissing each side of her collarbone and sending a frisson of pleasure down her spine.

"Mmm," was all Megan said.

Denver took her hand. Her dress fell to the floor around her feet and she left it there, a puddle of scarlet floral cotton.

Denver pushed the hair back from her face. "First course, this way."

"What about *actual* dinner?" Megan asked. They'd returned to the living room, relieved to find Denver's well-trained dogs hadn't eaten the cheese or knocked over the champagne. "Whatever you're making smells delicious."

"Roast chicken, mashed potatoes, fresh peas, and a wonderful kale spanakopita I scored from the Washington Acres café."

Megan punched his arm lightly. "Did Alvaro make the entire meal?"

Denver feigned offense. "Hardly. I'll have you know I made the chicken and the peas. Alvaro may have kicked in the potatoes."

"I'm sure it will be delicious."

They chatted over dinner in his dining room, avoiding the topics he'd said were off limits. When they were finished, he topped off the champagne in each flute and brought out the dessert—a berry crisp.

"With ice cream?" Megan asked.

"Is there any other way to eat it? Then a movie, if you'll stay."

"I'll stay."

By the time Megan left, it was almost midnight. She was feeling full and happy and grateful to escape reality, if for a little while.

But when she pulled into her driveway, she saw the light on in the parlor. That meant Bibi was still up. Maybe they could have a conversation that was long overdue.

The house was quiet, though. Bibi was asleep on her recliner in much the same position she'd been in earlier in the day. Sadie was curled in a ball by the chair, and Gunther and Sarge were lying by the stairs, probably wondering why their charge hadn't gone up for the night.

"Come on, Bibi," Megan whispered. She touched her grandmother's arm lightly. "If you sleep here, you'll get a stiff neck."

Bibi murmured something unintelligible before opening her eyes. When she saw Megan, she smiled. "How was your date?"

"Wonderful."

"I'm so glad."

"Come on, I'll help you up the steps."

It took them fifteen minutes to make it to the top. "I'm sorry," Bibi said when they got to her bedroom. "You must be tired. Sometimes my legs just don't cooperate. They get so stiff."

Megan sat on her grandmother's bed. "Is that why you have the painkiller prescriptions?"

"You saw that."

"You didn't exactly hide them. Why didn't you tell me? And what's this about you and Gertie going to see Serenity Manor? It sounds like the name for a cemetery."

Both she and Bibi laughed.

"It really does," Bibi said.

"Don't you want to live here anymore? This is your house. You raised a family here."

"It's *only* a house, Megan. Remember that. Houses don't matter. Stuff doesn't matter." She yawned. "*People* matter." She sat next to Megan on the bed, easing herself down with obvious discomfort. "And I don't *want* to leave. I'm a practical woman. You know that. If this house isn't working for me, I owe it to myself to at least explore other options. Gertie and some others were looking at Serenity. Nice place, but not for me." She made a face. "You can't have a crockpot. Can you imagine me without a crockpot?"

"No, Bibi, I can't." She pushed a hair back from her grandmother's face. How long would they have together? The thought brought about an ache in her chest. "I can't imagine you not here, either."

"Well, you don't have to. I'm not ready for Serenity Manor. I am, however, ready for sleep. Speaking of Gertie, I endured two hours of Gertie reminiscing about her husband, a litigator in the city. How smart he was, how dapper. How he'd go after the big companies when no one else would. I didn't mind the first thirty minutes, but after that it got old."

Only Megan was no longer listening. In a flash, she understood the connection between her and Penny Greenleaf.

"Good night, Bibi," she said hurriedly. "I have to take care of something before I go to bed."

Back in her room, she looked up those names again. She knew why they were in Penny's file next to her own. She knew what the number 3 on the paper Merry had found meant as well.

She called King's number. This time he answered.

"Do you know how late it is, Megan?"

"I know why Penny was looking for me. I can't believe I missed it before."

"You have my attention."

Megan carried the cell phone to the window. She looked out on the farm, at the light Porter had on in the Marshall house barn. Her next words would give her no sense of victory.

"My first year out of law school, well before I came to Winsome, I was an associate on a big case. It was a class action suit that had dragged on for years. The plaintiffs alleged that a company had recklessly used a toxic chemical in the plant. People died, others suffered irreversible side effects. It was ugly. There was lots of evidence, but the company got off on a technicality. A technicality the law firm I worked for unearthed." Megan lowered her voice. "A technicality I discovered."

"Oh, wow—"

"The company settled for a pittance. The men on that list were plaintiffs in the case. I bet if we scrub that list, Penny's father was on there, too—or his wife was, as his representative."

"Megan—"

"Claire's father died when she was young," the words were coming out in a jumble now. "Penny mothered her. Finding me must have been some sort of revenge, some type of closure."

"How could Penny have known?"

"I'm sure she didn't know I'd found the technicality. But Penny was an amateur sleuth. She loved mysteries, loved projects, loved her family. She must have seen my name on some of the documentation and knew I'd been involved. There were three attorneys from the firm. I was the third." Megan paused. "I said there are no coincidences, Bobby, but I think this may very well be one."

"The fact that you live in the same town where the memorial was held?"

"Yes. She had her chance to speak with me." Megan remembered the look she'd given her at the Indian restaurant. Simmering rage. Now Megan knew why. "Only she died before she could confront me."

"Her burial on your property?"

"Clearly someone else knew about her vendetta."

"Olive?" King asked.

"I'm thinking Claire."

"*Claire?*"

"Penny felt bad for Claire after all she's been through. I met Evan, I've seen his lifestyle firsthand. I know how Claire was living."

"You visited Evan?"

Megan ignored the question. "Claire knows about Penny. She knows Penny can be obsessive about a cause. She probably wanted Penny off her back. You said it yourself, she was still in love with David."

"Maybe it's just late, Megan, and I'm not thinking straight, but that doesn't seem like enough to kill your own sister."

"What if a big inheritance was at stake? What if you were plotting to get rid of your competition and your sister found out. Remember, Penny was buried with the flowers. The last person to see that bouquet was Claire."

"A big inheritance. You mean the crazy will Martin set up."

"You knew?"

"We talked to his lawyers this afternoon. They said Martin

wanted Dominick to choose between David and Claire."

"And submit back-up for his decision. Yes, I talked to Dom. He really got the crappy end of things. Here's what I've been thinking." Megan forced herself to slow down, realizing she sounded manic. "Claire has everything to lose. The house. The money. The prestige. She's already lost David. What if she plotted against Melanie and was found out? She goes into hiding, but her sister, the unstoppable sleuth, has already put five and five together. Penny confronts Claire, things get heated, and one thing leads to another."

Megan could hear commotion on King's end of the line. "Clover's kicking me out of the room," King said. "Give me a minute." Megan heard him shuffling around, and then in a quieter voice, he said, "What I don't understand is how she got the body to your place. Even if she took Penny there to throw suspicion your way knowing that Penny had been researching you, how would she have physically moved her sister?"

"An accomplice."

"Who would that be?"

"The man who is missing. The man who could easily carry Penny. The man Claire was looking for at Gertie's house." Megan took a breath, forced herself to slow down. "The man who was seen at the von Tressler estate." Megan filled King in on her trip to the city. "Claire and Duke Masterman. Both single."

"I don't know—"

"And when I told Evan I'd met Claire in Winsome, he didn't react at all. If she had only gone for the memorial, you'd think he would have questioned our relationship. But he knows Claire came here often."

"To see Duke."

"And plan."

King was quiet for a moment. "How would she have met Duke?"

That bothered Megan, too. There were a few things that still bothered her. Like where Olive fit in. "Maybe Claire reached out to him. She knew he had access to David and Melanie's property. Perhaps she promised him a chunk of change if he cooperated." Or a house. A very big house. *He acts like he owns the place*, the landscaper had said. "Porter said he's a gambler. He may have needed cash."

King sighed loudly into the phone. "This all sounds right in theory, Megan, but I need to do more research."

"Can you get a warrant for the house in Chestnut Hill? I bet you'll find Claire—or at least evidence she's been living there."

"I don't have enough for a warrant, Megan. You know that." King yawned. "I have meetings in the morning, but I'll be around in the afternoon. Call me then."

Megan slipped her phone on the charger and brushed her teeth. She lay in bed beside Sadie thinking about her evening with Denver. She missed him, and she'd broken all of his rules once she returned home.

Staying with him would have been nice. Having him here? Even better.

Megan turned onto her side. She replayed her conversations with Dom, Evan, Gertie, Olive, and Melanie over and over again. What was she missing? Her theory about Claire felt right, but she was sure there was some critical piece to this puzzle.

Sadie began snoring softly and Megan stroked her head. "Sleep, old friend," she whispered. Someone should get some rest. She knew sleep would not come easily for her.

Twenty-Five

Serenity Manor seemed to be all the brochure promised it would. Ten rolling acres in bucolic Bucks County. A beautiful dining area, topnotch food, a gym, hair salon, five-lane pool, art studio, and even a cat room for those who missed their pets. One-floor apartments equipped with a kitchen alcove and separate bedroom. Bright, modern—and blandly institutional.

"Not bad, right?" Jenny Clark said.

Jenny had the enthusiasm and perspective of a twenty-year-old raised in the comfortable suburbs, and Megan wanted to take her at her word. But she knew marketing and reality weren't always the same. The residents *looked* happy. Were they happy?

"Ask a few yourself. We're going to grab coffee in the cafeteria. See how they interact."

"Is it true you can't have crockpots?"

"Or curling irons, or space heaters, or toaster ovens, or a number of other small appliances," Jenny said. "It is strict that way. And no dogs."

Bibi without dogs. The thought saddened Megan.

Megan followed her hostess to a table in the middle of the dining area. Jenny left and returned with two coffees and a basket of brownie bites. "I always eat their brownies. They're the best. And the residents can have all they want."

Oh, lord, Megan thought. Bibi with access to unlimited sweets.

"Why did you want to talk to me, Megan?"

Megan swirled her coffee around with a metal spoon. "As I'm sure you've guessed, I didn't come here for the grand tour—although I appreciated it. I understand you worked the memorial at the von Tressler estate."

Jenny put her coffee down without drinking. "Did I do something wrong?" A petite girl with large dark eyes and a mop of brown curls, she looked nervous.

"No, no. I just have a few questions about what went on. You see, a woman is missing. I dropped her off at the memorial, but she never showed up. I was wondering if you saw her. Her name is Claire von Tressler."

Megan slid a photo she'd gotten off the internet across the table. Jenny stared at it for a few seconds before sliding it back.

"Sorry, I've never seen her before."

"You're sure?"

Jenny glanced at the photo again. "You have to understand, the caterer was very stern with all of us. No fraternizing, and it was crowded at times. I didn't really talk to anyone. Is it possible she was there? I guess, but I think I would have noticed."

"How about this man?" Megan handed her a photo of Dom, the one from LinkedIn.

"Yes, him I saw. He was talking to Melanie and Veronica at one point. I don't think he stayed long."

"But you didn't see Claire? She wasn't with them—you're certain?"

"No, I'm sorry."

"It's okay. I appreciate your help." Megan pulled the photos together and put them back in her bag.

"I did overhear Melanie talking about her, if that means

anything."

Megan was in the middle of closing her purse. She paused. "Do you remember what she was saying?"

"Not really. She was talking with a guy in what I think was the study. Lots of bookshelves, no books. I thought maybe that's what you wanted to talk about." Her skin flushed red. "I was looking for a spot to take a call, and I kind of opened the door on them. Melanie was pretty angry."

"Were they doing something they shouldn't have been doing?"

Jenny's eyes grew wide. "Oh, goodness, no. I guess I just interrupted their discussion, and she was annoyed. I heard Claire's name mentioned as I was opening the door."

"Do you remember what the man looked like?"

"I can do better. I know who he is. My uncle has used him for work now and again. Duke Masterman. He lives on Canal Street down the road from your café." Jenny's gaze strayed to the table beside them. "Uncle Roger says he was doing work for Melanie, so that makes sense." She peered at Megan. "Right?"

Megan agreed. She thanked Jenny again and left, managing to get to her car without running. She had been wrong all along. She needed to talk with King.

But first, she dialed Ryan's number as fast as she could. She had a hunch, and he could give it credence. He picked up immediately.

"What's up, Megan?"

"Last Thursday morning, were you working on my house?"

"Are you okay? You don't sound so good. You're breathing hard."

"I'm fine, I just need to know. It's important."

"Hold on, let me check." Ryan was back on the line in two minutes. "June 30, right? No, I wasn't here. I had some other work to do."

"Do you remember where you were?"

"I came back here in the afternoon. In the morning...let's see. I stopped by the Myers first thing in the morning to fix their garage door. Mr. Myers is my mom's friend and he was having a fit because their door was stuck open. Afraid of burglars. Quick fix for me. After that...hold on, checking...I stopped at the von Tressler's property to work on the basement. You know that Duke had left parts of the job unfinished, and water was coming in through a hole in the wall when it rained."

"Did you fix the hole?"

"I did."

"Was your presence really needed?"

"The hole needed to be fixed, if that's what you're asking. The carpet was wet down there, and I could see where water had leaked in. Personally, Melanie let it go too long, but with David's passing, I guess she had other things on her mind."

"This is important, Ryan, so take your time. Was Melanie there when you were?"

"I don't need to take my time. The answer is no. I had to deal with her mother, Veronica. A real sweetheart."

Megan thanked her contractor and hung up. Her next call was to King. He didn't answer—meetings all morning, she recalled—so she left an urgent message. It took him seconds to call her back.

"I'm tied up, Megan. Can it wait?"

"No."

"Executive summary then."

Megan forced her breathing to slow down. "I was wrong. It's not Claire you want. It's Melanie."

"Melanie? I thought she was the next target. Competition for the estate and all."

"Right, that's what I thought. But today I spoke with someone who saw Duke at the memorial gathering."

"So?"

"Duke was supposed to be missing. Why was he at the memorial?"

"To repay what he owed."

"Melanie claims he never did that. She claims he hasn't been seen in weeks."

"Who saw him? Someone reliable?"

"Jenny Clark, Roger's niece. She was working the memorial. She knows Duke, says she walked in on Melanie and Duke talking in a room together."

"Megan, hold on—"

"There's more. You asked me what Ryan was doing the morning Penny was killed. Ryan was at the von Tressler estate— *at Melanie's request.*" She paused. "And Melanie wasn't there."

Dead air. "Bobby? Don't you see, it adds up. Claire wasn't coming to Winsome to be with Duke, she was coming to be with David. They continued their affair. Meanwhile, Melanie was getting it on with Duke. She and Duke decided to kill Claire after David died. Kill the competition. I bet Penny overheard them planning ways to get rid of her, and they killed her to silence her. She had information about me in her possession, so it was easy enough to place her body on my property."

King said, "And then Claire ran."

"She knew her life was in danger. Maybe she saw something at the memorial. She's been lurking around, though. Checked up on Duke by posing as a cop."

"I had my officers drive by Duke's house. Empty. As you said, the neighbors haven't seen him in weeks. Still think he's staying at the Chestnut Hill property?"

Megan thought about the sequence of events. "That would

be my guess."

"We'll work with the Philadelphia police department to get a drive by, check it out. In the meantime, just go home. Please? If what you say is right, and if Melanie suspects you're on to her, you could be a target."

Megan had thought the same thing. "She probably hired Clay to check up on me. See what I know."

"Likely." He said something to someone in the room with him. "Megan, I have to go. I'll call you later. Again, go home. Stay there. Please."

Twenty-Six

Megan arrived back at the farm at lunchtime. She was surprised to see Bibi's car in the driveway along with another—one she didn't recognize. One of her Bridge friends, perhaps, Megan thought. Or a woman from their church. She could see Clay and Porter milling around in the back fields, and she heard hammering at the Marshall house. She was glad to be home.

Inside, the house was oddly quiet. The dogs were up at the barn with Clay, Megan figured—normal for a nice day. The kitchen smelled of cinnamon and coffee, and the dishes in the sink said Bibi was entertaining. The murmur of voices drifted from the parlor.

"Megan, is that you?" Bibi called.

"It is. I'll be there in a moment."

"Bring me some hot tea, please. Black tea would be nice."

"Okay," Megan replied.

Hot tea? There were two cups in the sink and two dessert plates, which meant Bibi had already had coffee and cake. She *never* had more than one cup of caffeine in the afternoon, and her typical tea was chamomile. Black tea was caffeinated.

You're overthinking this, Megan told herself. She boiled water and put the water and teabag in a Winsome mug. Pausing by the kitchen door, Megan held her breath so she could hear what was going on in the parlor. The murmuring had stopped.

Something was wrong. One, Bibi could always be heard chattering when she had guests. Two, Bibi usually bustled in to meet Megan when she got home, guest or no guest. Three, the tea.

Four, the car outside was a Mercedes. Who did they know who drove a Mercedes? No one.

Megan figured the tea was some kind of Bibi signal. "Cream?" she yelled to her grandmother.

"Definitely!" was her perky response.

That cemented it. Bibi didn't believe in milk products in her tea, and she knew Megan knew that. Definitely a signal. Quickly, Megan banged some drawers to make it sound like she was getting a spoon for the tea. She shoved a paring knife up the sleeve of her blouse. She texted King that something was amiss, and she was about to text Clay to come down to the house with Gunther when she felt a presence behind her.

"Hello, Dom," she said, her back to the door.

"How did you know?" he asked pleasantly. "Were you expecting me to call on your grandmother?"

Megan turned to face him, keeping the arm with the knife behind her back. She saw the same serious young man she'd met at Starbucks, only this time he was holding a gun and pointing it at her.

"Where's my grandmother?"

"Put the tea and your phone down and I'll show you." He smiled. "She's fine. A little tied up right now, you might say."

Megan placed the tea on the counter and yelled, "Bibi!"

"I'm fine, Megan," came her grandmother's voice from the other room.

"You don't trust me, the golden boy of von Tressler Investments? I'm disappointed. And after I spent so much time sharing my boo-hoo story with you." Dom walked closer. "So how did you know it was me? Tell me, please. I like a game as much as my grandfather did. I thought we were pretty careful."

"You were," Megan said. "Until I saw the Mercedes, I thought Melanie was working with Duke Masterman. But as I was making the tea—which my grandmother would never ask for after having coffee, by the way, especially with cream—I realized I was missing an even bigger picture. Claire was still bedding David, right?"

Dom nodded.

"And Melanie was sleeping with the help—Duke, that is, right?"

Another nod.

"For Melanie and Duke, the immediate problem wasn't Claire, it was David. That's where you came in."

The amused look on Dom's face dimmed slightly. "Go on."

"David was a problem all around. He stood between Melanie and her boy toy. He stood between you and ownership of the company. With that prenup in place, he stood between Melanie and freedom. And he wouldn't ditch that girlfriend of his, Claire. You and Melanie decided to kill David, which was oh-so-easy given his preexisting heart issues. A little of the right poison, and no one would ever know a thing."

"A good story so far." Dom waved the gun. "Go on."

The kitchen was warm, and Megan was sweating. She blinked away sweat that had dripped into her eyes.

"I said go on."

"The problem was, once David was gone, you had a distraught Claire to contend with. And even worse, Claire's big sister Penelope, a woman who valued family loyalty above all else. Penny overheard you and Melanie plotting at the memorial, and she confronted you. The next day, you and Melanie took care of that issue—with a little help from a certain contractor. Putting Penny's body on my property was a no brainer. She'd been asking about me all around town, so you could throw the police off the trail by having them chase shadows."

Dom began to clap using his gun as the other hand. "Impressive."

"I'm not sure how you and Melanie got together. Maybe an affair of your own—keeping it in the family and all. Maybe you had a little tête-à-tête during a family dinner and realized how much you both hated the von Tresslers."

"Maybe we both just hated David."

"Maybe. Only now you had two people to get rid of. One, Claire. With her dead, Melanie would be set to inherit everything. I'm sure the two of you made some type of deal keeping you on as CEO and eventually transferring more ownership to you. A real win-win. Two," Megan met his gaze. The knife felt heavy against her arm, and she fought to keep it steady as she let it fall into her sweaty hand. "Two, Duke. He'd served his purpose, and now he was a liability."

"This is all wonderful, and quite astute of you to figure it all out so eloquently, but you have no proof. David's been cremated, and his official cause of death states natural causes. And Duke? He's a womanizer who frequently disappears. No one will miss him."

"You're forgetting something."

A shadow crossed Dom's features. "What's that?"

"Me." Megan hurled the knife across the room. It grazed Dom's cheek and clipped a chunk off his ear. In the moment he took to recover, he dropped the gun. Megan sprang across the room, flinging herself onto Dom. He was a small man, but strong. She used her elbows to dig into his neck while her fingernails clawed at his eyes. Bibi was shouting from the other room. Megan could hear sirens in the distance and dogs barking outside.

Dom struggled to sit up. Megan used whatever leverage she could to throw herself against him.

He gasped. She dug her elbows in harder, feeling soft flesh give way under her body. Blood soaked the floor by his head. His hands were pulling at her, but she felt an adrenaline rush like never before. He was in *her* home, and *her* grandmother was tied up in the other room. She pressed harder. His struggling stopped.

Megan stared down at the man underneath her, afraid to let up.

The kitchen door slammed open. Porter and Clay rushed in alongside Gunther and Sarge. The dogs barked and growled at the man on the floor.

Clay picked up the gun.

"Stand down," Porter told Sarge, who was dangerously close to Dom's face.

"You can get up, Megan," Clay said. He tugged at her arm gently, the arm that was still digging into Dom's neck. "He's passed out from the pressure. Let up or you'll kill him."

Drained, Megan rolled off Dom. She looked up at Clay and Porter. "Bibi," she said, winded. "Parlor."

"I think King's here." Clay kept the gun aimed at the unconscious man while Porter went to release Bibi. "We heard Bonnie screaming. I don't know what the hell happened, but I'm glad you're okay."

"Me, too," Megan said. "I might not have been if it weren't for Bibi and her rules about caffeine and tea."

Twenty-Seven

"We have an APB out for Melanie's arrest," King told Megan. They were sitting in a conference room at the police station, and King was taking her statement. "Don't worry, Megan, we'll find her." King looked at her with concern. "Do you know how Dominick even knew where you lived?"

"Wouldn't be hard to find. He knew Penny's body was found at the Marshall property. Wouldn't take much to find Washington Acres." Megan cradled her head with her hand. The headache that had been threatening for days was on full force. "What he planned to do here, I don't know."

"We think he planned to take Bonnie and use her as bait to get you to come to him. We found more rope and chloroform in his car." King's frown deepened. "He was going to scare you—or kill you."

Megan nodded. "Hopefully, he'll be away for hood." She had hit the video record button on her phone when she sensed Dom come into the kitchen, and King had listened to their exchange three times.

"Unfortunately, he doesn't really admit to anything beyond working with Melanie and hating David," King said. "But we'll place this into evidence. If we can find Melanie or Duke—"

"I think Duke is dead."

"How can you be so certain?"

"I'm not certain, but think about it. Originally, I thought Duke and Melanie were working alone, but Dom's involvement changes things. Dom has the real power here. What good does having a knucklehead like Duke around do for them? He's a partier and womanizer with a history of gambling. He was probably enticed by the promise of wealth to help Melanie carry out her plans. After that, useless. Worse, not trustworthy."

"We've checked his house. His car is missing." King looked skeptical. "I sent two of our best down to Chestnut Hill to look there."

Megan's head was pounding, but the mention of the Chestnut Hill house sparked Megan's memory. Megan looked up. "I think I know where you will find his body."

King looked at her quizzically. "Where?"

"There's a small, stinky pond on the Chestnut Hill property. Denver thought it was once a small fish pond, a little bigger than a coffin, but deep and full of goop—dead leaves and branches. A body weighted down well might never be discovered. At least not until someone moves into the house and tries to clean out the pond."

"Like the killers," King said. "If Dominick and Melanie dump Duke's body, then get possession of the house, they would never have to worry he would be found."

"Right. A perfect crime. At least in the eyes of a psychopath."

"Or a pair of psychopaths."

One of King's officers entered the small room. "Chief, we need you for a moment."

King nodded curtly. "Can I get you anything, Megan?"

"Maybe Tylenol? And an update on my grandmother?"

King smiled. "Done."

*   *   *

King returned with Denver, two Tylenol, a glass of water, and an update on Bibi.

"Bonnie's been checked out by a paramedic. She's fine. Feisty as ever."

"Thanks, Bobby." Megan accepted the glass of water and swallowed the painkillers.

"And we have some good news." King pulled up a seat at the table. He exchanged a knowing look with Denver. "We found Melanie."

Megan's shoulders relaxed in relief. "At her mother's?"

King said, "Close. En route. The APB had provided details on both her and her mom's cars. Dom must have tipped Melanie off. She and Veronica were caught about a half hour away from Veronica's house."

"Think the mother was involved?" Denver asked.

"It's possible she knew what was happening, but we don't think she was part of the planning."

"Getting Melanie to confess will be a Herculean feat," Megan said. "She's a good actress. I think she even bullshits herself."

"If we find Duke's body, that will make things easier. But there's still the issue of Claire."

"I know where she's staying," Megan said softly. It was something she'd been thinking about for a while. "Remember I saw the light in the house in Philly?" Megan said to Denver. When he nodded, she said, "I thought it was Claire who was squatting there. But you were right—for her, that would be a house of ghosts."

"It was Duke?" King asked.

"Yes. Claire's been staying with her brother, Evan. He'll

deny it. I went there and the place was a mess, but what better cover for a neat freak like Claire?'

"We'll check it out."

"She may come forward before you find her. Especially once she finds out Melanie and Dom are in custody." Megan sipped the water. It tasted metallic.

"I hope so," King said.

"While your officers are there, take the CDs from her room."

King tilted his head. "CDs?"

"I have a hunch, Bobby. Evan mentioned that his sister had left behind 'worthless CDs.' I believe Melanie and Dom conspired to kill David—"

King interrupted, "It's difficult to prove he was murdered, not without a body or a confession, and right now the latter looks unlikely and the former is in ashes in an urn underground."

"If you have strong enough proof of planning coupled with a body and strong motive, it may be enough," Megan said. "If you find Claire and have witness testimony, even better."

"What do you think those CDs contain?" Denver asked.

"I don't know, but why keep them if they're not important? She kept nothing else."

Twenty-Eight

It felt good to be home with Bibi and Denver. It felt even better knowing Dom and Melanie were in custody. The fact that Dom had come here to their home unnerved Megan, but she had, in effect, led him here. Had she never reached out to talk with him, he might not have bothered with her. She put Bibi at risk, and she wasn't sure she could forgive herself for that.

At the same time, had Dom not come, he'd still be at large. With Melanie in Winsome, who knew what problems they could have caused.

"Ultimately, it was a blessing," Bibi said. "That man never hurt me. As a matter of fact, we had a lovely talk over cake and coffee before you arrived. Then I invited him to wait in the parlor. Of course, when the gun came out, I knew he wasn't so nice."

"Why'd he tie you up?" Denver asked.

"I may have tried to hit him with a plate."

"Oh, Bibi." Megan shook her head.

"Don't laugh. It was your great-grandmother's best cake plate. The one with a heavy base. Would have made a mighty dent if he hadn't wrestled it away."

Megan had put together a simple salad, and they were eating it with a loaf of Bibi's sourdough bread and some cheese. Denver had brought wine, and he poured a glass for himself and

Megan. Bibi declined.

"The bit about the tea was brilliant." Megan shared the story with Denver. "I knew she wouldn't ask for black tea after coffee."

"He told me to act normal!"

"Well, once you accepted cream in your tea, I knew we were in trouble."

Denver sat back and refolded his napkin on his lap. "You too know each other well."

Megan smiled at her grandmother. *We sure do.*

"How about hosting that grand opening?" Denver asked. "This Saturday. Ryan says the house is mostly finished. Porter is out of the barn. Clay, Porter, and I can help you and Bibi get ready."

"The town could use the celebration," Bibi said.

Megan was tired. Bone tired. But a celebration sounded good.

"Only if we keep it simple. *Very* simple."

Bibi nodded. "Simple it is."

When they were finished doing dishes, after Denver had left to attend to his dogs and dusk had fallen in Winsome, Bibi tugged on Megan's arm.

"Can we go for a walk?" she asked.

"Now, Bibi? It's late. I'm tired, you must be tired." When Bibi didn't back down, Megan said, "Fine. A walk."

Megan waited while her grandmother put on her sneakers. Bibi was wearing linen drawstring pants and a "Winsome Proud" rainbow shirt, a leftover from Megan's father's souvenir shop so many years ago. She looked tiny and frail to Megan tonight.

"How about your cane?" Megan said.

"Don't need it. I have you." She grabbed a keyring out of a kitchen drawer.

Megan and Bibi, with Gunther and Sadie following, headed into the yard.

"Are we going somewhere in particular?"

"You'll see."

Megan felt a flutter of anxiety, but she quelled it. Killers were behind bars, Bibi was out moving about—it was a good night. They walked past the barn, past the outdoor patio, past the greenhouses, and to the fields that separated the Washington Acres property and the old Marshall property.

"Look what Ryan and Porter did," Bibi said.

Where there had been a muddy meadow between the two properties, a stone path now led the way from the farm to the restored Marshall house. The men had leveled the area. They'd put down simple pavers, with a few feet mowed on either side—enough to walk comfortably, even in the dark.

"It looks amazing," Megan said, awed. While she had been running around after the von Tresslers, the men had conspired to do this.

"My gift to you," Bibi said.

Megan hugged her grandmother. "I love it."

"There's something else."

Megan followed Bibi across the pathway and to the Marshall house. Their progress was slow but steady. Once at the house, Bibi unlocked the front door with the keyring she'd pocketed back at the farm. She opened the door, flipped on the light, and led Megan inside.

The entry looked just as it had when Ryan had showed it to her, only now it was pristine. Walls wiped down, floors mopped, windows washed. Ryan did nice work.

"This way." Bibi went through the kitchen—also immaculately clean now—and stopped at the door to the caretaker apartment. She used a different key to open this door.

Megan entered behind her grandmother. It looked the same as last time she'd seen it: spacious and modern and bright. Bibi walked through the main living area and into the bedroom. She opened the bathroom door and pointed to the shower. Grab bars had been installed along the rear wall.

"Good idea," Megan said.

"Ryan did that for me."

Megan blinked, unsure what her grandmother was telling her. "Why?"

"This is where I want to live. It's perfect, Megan. One floor. At the farm. Near you, but I'll have my own space."

Central air, zoned heating, a pretty view...Megan could see the appeal.

"You'll be alone."

"You'll be a few seconds away. Plus, Ryan's putting an alarm system in."

"You hate alarm systems."

"If it means my independence, and it makes you happy, I'm all for them." Bibi smiled. "I told you I would tell you when I need something. I need something." When Megan didn't respond, Bibi said, "Look, the doc says my joints are old and I'm riddled with arthritis. That's not going to improve. I don't want a lift on the steps at the farmhouse, and I don't want to lose my parlor to a makeshift bedroom. I don't want to be coddled or treated like a child."

"Bibi, I—"

"Not that you've done any of those things. Well, maybe occasionally." Another smile. "I want to be with you, but I also want to be independent. Here, I can be useful. I can man the front desk, teach bread-making, greet guests. You don't have to pay me. I have a nice kitchen, all the amenities, and I can come and go as I please. You'll be here when I need you." She put her hands on small hips. "And no stairs."

Megan felt her eyes stinging. Before she knew it, warm tears were spilling down her face.

"If you don't want me to,—" Bibi sounded alarmed.

Megan shook her head. She leaned up against the wall and put her head back. The anxiety and concern of the prior weeks came pouring out, and she sobbed until she felt dry and empty.

Once she had herself together, Megan hugged her grandmother.

"You're okay with this, Megan? I'm not ruining your plans?"

"I think it's a grand idea."

"You'll always be welcome."

"It'll be an adjustment."

Bibi nodded. "And maybe Sadie can visit me from time to time."

"Any time you like."

"It's settled then," Bibi said. She took Megan's hand, stroked the side of her face. "Now you may have to carry me back to the farm. That was a long walk."

Megan squeezed her hand. "Something tells me you'll be just fine."

Twenty-Nine

The call from King came Thursday night, after Megan and Bibi had gone to bed.

"Did I wake you?"

Yes. "No, no...what's up, Bobby? Did you find Claire?" After everything, including her own tragic connection to the family's deceased father, Megan felt a certain responsibility for Claire, one she couldn't shake.

"Not yet. But I thought you'd want to know that you called it—well, mostly."

Megan waited. This was news she knew was coming, but she'd been anxious to hear, nonetheless."

"Duke's remains were recovered at the Philly house."

"In the little fishpond?"

"Some of him was there, yes. Some parts were found in fresh graves in the on-site cemetery."

Megan digested the awful gruesomeness of those statements. "Which means he'd been killed pretty recently, after Denver and I were there, anyway. It had been dark, but I think we would have noticed fresh dirt in that tiny area." She closed her eyes, thinking of her former contractor. "I'm sorry to hear this."

"I was too."

"How about the CDs? Anything useful?"

"It took me most of today to get a warrant, which is why I'm calling so late. We searched Evan's house. At first he stuck to his story that Claire hadn't been there in weeks, but when we gently reminded him that he's on parole and lying to the police could land him back in the slammer, suddenly his tune changed."

"She has been crashing there."

"Yes. There, and with Olive."

"So Olive knew all along. She pointed a finger at me to protect Claire."

King yawned. "Sorry, been up for almost twenty-four hours. At first Olive thought you were involved because of the material on Penny's computer, but eventually Claire reached out to her. After that, she continued to keep up the search façade just to protect her sister. She was relieved to find out Melanie and Dom had been caught."

Megan could see that. Olive and Penny were, if nothing else, protective. She said, "The family seemed to genuinely take care of one another."

"Which made it harder for me to sort through the lies and almost-lies. I owe you my gratitude."

Megan smiled. "I have your back." She repositioned herself in bed. Sadie stretched, yawned, and went back to sleep—not an apparent care in the world. "The CDs?"

"I was getting to that. We took them. You were right. They're tapes transferred to CDs, and what's on those tapes would be incriminating to Melanie and Dominick."

"Would be?"

"From what we can tell, and we're still reviewing them, David must have gotten wind that Melanie and his nephew were plotting against him in order to split the business. He installed tapes and video cameras throughout the new house. We have footage of Melanie and Duke, as well as hours of recorded conversations between Melanie and Dominick."

Thinking like a litigator, Melanie said, "But he recorded them without their knowledge or permission, so you're thinking the tapes are inadmissible."

"Bingo. The tapes make it clear that they planned to do away with David. With David out of the way, Melanie would be a better choice than Claire. And if Claire was pinned for her sister's murder—or killed—then there was no choice to make at all."

"And the stone through Melanie's window?"

"Could have been Melanie, trying to set the stage that Claire was behind this. Could have been a random act like your grandmother's tire."

Megan thought back to the Philly house, to the content of those CDs. "So poor Duke was never in it for the long term, whether or not he wanted to be."

"A happy idiot—isn't that what they're called? Melanie convinced him he would get rich. Disposed of him when he'd outlived his usefulness." A pause. "Again, you were right."

"That's no consolation. Three people are dead."

"And at least one is still alive, thanks to you."

Mother Nature graced them with sunshine, mild temperatures, and a cool breeze on Saturday morning. The Marshall barn had been set up for a baking demonstration, Alvaro's treats— homemade soft pretzels, cups of freshly-popped popcorn, cookies, and plates of fresh vegetables and dips—were set out in the barn classroom, and the Marshall house itself, officially christened as the "Marshall House Retreat," was mostly furnished and open for tours, working plumbing included.

"Still worried that people will come here just to see a crime scene?" Clay asked.

Megan gave him a toothy smile. "Not at all."

Whatever their reason for attending, the crowds started rolling in at noon, after the farmers market. Bibi sat at the reception desk Ryan had built and handed out information about the Retreat's offerings. Clay and Porter kept the food coming and the garbage cleared, while Clover painted children's faces. Even Gunther and Sadie were in residence. It was everything Megan could do to keep Gunther from herding the children.

"You did well," Megan told Ryan, who'd joined the festivities with most of his crew. "And thank you for all the special touches for my grandmother. I suspect you built that innkeeper's quarters with her in mind."

Ryan simply smiled.

By two, the crowds had grown sparse. The food was nearly gone, and Clover's queue was down to three little boys.

Megan grabbed Denver's hand. "I want to show you something. Come with me."

She led him around the back of the barn where they had a view of the Pennsylvania hillside. The sky was clear lapis lazuli, the trees a sharp green contrast against the horizon. Fields of yellow flowers dotted the meadows. It felt like a perfect summer day.

"It's gorgeous," Denver said, looking out at the vista.

When he turned back, Megan was down on one knee. "Marry me, Daniel Finn."

Denver's eyes widened in surprised before his face gave way to a look of pure joy that made Megan's heart soar. She'd known for a while this was the right path. It had just taken her time to realize it.

"Are ye sure, Megs? Absolutely certain?"

"Marry me, Denver. I'm absolutely certain."

"On your knee and everything. Wait until I tell my sister."

"Is that a 'yes'? Can I get up now—or are you going to leave me on the ground?"

Denver picked her up and spun her around. "It's a yes, Megs. It's very definitely a yes."

Megan was halfway down the path to the farm, near the largest greenhouse, when she heard a rustling behind her. Sadie stopped and growled. Megan was carrying supplies back to the house, and she spun around, half expecting to see Dominick. Instead, the woman who stood before her was small and brunette—with killer cheekbones.

"Claire."

Claire smiled wanly. No designer threads today—just jeans and a pink t-shirt. Brown hair was pulled back in a stubby ponytail. Her hands were empty and open.

Sadie relaxed, and Megan did, too.

"I'm here to thank you." Claire flushed. "And to apologize."

"For what?"

"When you left me off at the memorial, I knew I couldn't actually go in. David had left me a package buried under the potting shed. He'd left it there in case something happened to him. I slashed our tire so I could arrive ahead of my sisters. Once I found it, I knew I wasn't safe. I never thought my sisters would focus on you." Her face darkened. "I never thought Penny would be in danger."

"I'm sorry about Penny."

"No one is sorrier than I am."

Megan nodded. "You did what you had to."

Claire's smile didn't reach her eyes. "Is the police chief

here?"

"Bobby King? Yes, he's at the barn. Come on, I'll walk you up. He'll be happy to see you."

As they walked side by side, Megan felt nothing but sorrow for her companion. To love a man forbidden to you, and to suffer all of this? Tragic. The tapes captured on those CDs would at least be worth more with Claire corroborating their content. Maybe justice would prevail. After what she and her family had been through, she deserved some justice.

"This is a lovely farm. You live here?"

"Down there, in the big farmhouse."

"Lucky you," Claire said.

"It's not the house that makes me lucky."

Megan could see her family talking in the distance. King had his arm around Clover, who was holding Emily's daughter in her arms. Emily and Clay were chatting with Bibi and Denver, who, Megan was sure, was busily spreading the news of their engagement. Alvaro was popping more popcorn in the machine they'd rented for the day, and the rich smells of the corn and butter were wafting this way.

Claire stopped short when they reached the end of the stone path.

"What's wrong?" Megan asked.

"They all look so...happy. I don't want to break it up."

Megan smiled. "You won't. Come on." She took the woman's hand. "You'll be welcome."

"Even after everything?"

Megan squeezed her hand. "Especially after everything."

Photo by Ian Pickarski

WENDY TYSON

Wendy Tyson's background in law and psychology has provided inspiration for her mysteries and thrillers. Originally from the Philadelphia area, Wendy lives in Vermont with her family and three dogs. Wendy's short fiction has appeared in literary journals and crime fiction anthologies, and she's a contributing editor and columnist for *The Big Thrill* and *The Thrill Begins*, International Thriller Writers' online magazines. Wendy is the author of the Allison Campbell Mystery Series and the Greenhouse Mystery Series.

The Greenhouse Mystery Series
by Wendy Tyson

Henery Press Mystery Books

And finally, before you go...
Here are a few other mysteries
you might enjoy:

PUMPKINS IN PARADISE

Kathi Daley

A Tj Jensen Mystery (#1)

Between volunteering for the annual pumpkin festival and coaching her girls to the state soccer finals, high school teacher Tj Jensen finds her good friend Zachary Collins dead in his favorite chair.

When the handsome new deputy closes the case without so much as a "why" or "how," Tj turns her attention from chili cook-offs and pumpkin carving to complex puzzles, prophetic riddles, and a decades-old secret she seems destined to unravel.

Available at booksellers nationwide and online

Visit www.henerypress.com for details

PILLOW STALK

Diane Vallere

A Madison Night Mystery (#1)

Interior Decorator Madison Night might look like a throwback to the sixties, but as business owner and landlord, she proves that independent women can have it all. But when a killer targets women dressed in her signature style—estate sale vintage to play up her resemblance to fave actress Doris Day—what makes her unique might make her dead.

The local detective connects the new crime to a twenty-year old cold case, and Madison's long-trusted contractor emerges as the leading suspect. As the body count piles up, Madison uncovers a Soviet spy, a campaign to destroy all Doris Day movies, and six minutes of film that will change her life forever.

Available at booksellers nationwide and online

Visit www.henerypress.com for details